Anne Manning

Passages in the life of the Faire Gospeller, Mistress Anne Askew

Anne Manning

Passages in the life of the Faire Gospeller, Mistress Anne Askew

ISBN/EAN: 9783337281915

Printed in Europe, USA, Canada, Australia, Japan

Cover: Foto ©Raphael Reischuk / pixelio.de

More available books at **www.hansebooks.com**

PASSAGES IN THE LIFE

OF

THE FAIRE GOSPELLER

MISTRESS ANNE ASKEW.

Recounted by yᵉ unworthie Pen of
Nicholas Moldwarp, B.A.,

AND NOW FIRST SET FORTH BY

THE AUTHOR OF "MARY POWELL."

Rather Death than falſe of Faith.

NEW YORK,
DODD, MEAD & COMPANY,
PUBLISHERS.

PASSAGES IN THE LIFE

OF

THE FAIRE GOSPELLER,

MISTRESS ANNE ASKEW.

CONTENTS.

—o—

SECTION VIII.

SECTION IX.

SECTION X.

SECTION XI.

SECTION XII.

SECTION XIII.

SECTION XIV.

SECTION XV.

SECTION XVI.

PROLOGUE.

What the Houſe Porter ſayd.

———— Yes, Sir, the Houſe hath a Blight
on it. I remember when 'twas not ſo . . .
that was when I was a Boy; and before you
were born, Sir. Not ſo very young? well,
you may be older than your favour, Sir . . .
In reſpect of years, I ſuppoſe I might be your
Grandfather, Sir.

Maybe ye come down to theſe parts for
fowling? Marry, we have decoys of teal,
widgeon, and others of the duck kind . . .
Greebes, goodwits, whimbrels, coots, ruffs an'
reeves find plenty of food in our filhy pools
and ſtreams. This county is a great reſort
of the feathered kind. Stares rooſt on the
reeds in winter, breaking 'em down by their
weight. *Not* a fowler, Sir?

. . . Stratford on Avòn, Sir? No, I've

never been there. I was born and bred on this land, Sir,—that's why I hang by it ftill. It has a bad name, folks fpeak ill of it, and I'm fure I've reafon to think ill of it ; but 'tis familiar to me, you fee. Well, it *is* low and fenny.

Ghofts, Sir? No! . . . I ne'er heed what they fay of 'em. There's none, Sir!—or there would be, here. Difmal Noifes there are, full fure, fighings of the Wind, and fo forth—fcurrying of Rats behind the Pannells,—creaks of ruftic Cafements,—old Furniture ftretching itfelf and yawning. Nothing worfe.

If I thought *fhe* walked, I'd watch the livelong Night for her, I warrant ye! But no, fhe's quiet where fhe is. There be others, might well be unquiet in their graves, but they would not haunt this place, Sir. Still, I deny not there be ftories about . . .

Now we come to Miftrefs Anne's picture. That's her.—Yes, it's like. 'Equal' to that, Sir? Blefs you!

This was done by an Italian. Her picture was painted in London, fome time after, but I doubt if by as good a hand. The other is called 'the motto picture.' This wants no

motto. I've feen her look juſt fo ; her lips a
little apart, ready to fpeak. That bad man
called her a parrot. ' Parrot ' quotha !

What did he mean by it? Well, Sir, he
meant to filence her; put her down. She
had too ſharp a wit for him : not ſharp i' th'
wrong fenfe, ye wot. Certes, when they
browbeat her, ſhe anſwered 'em agayn. A
worm will turn, Sir. Yes, Sir, juſt as you
fay : much enforced, ſhe would ſhow a haſty
fpark. Gone the next moment, Sir !

—If you look well at that picture, you'll
note there's not a ſingle hard line in it.
Maſter Moldwarp obferved it to me firſt. He
fayd there are no hard lines in nature, and
this picture is next to nature itfelf. Going—
you fee—before its time—the paint caking
off—covered with a network of ſmall cracks,
though painted in my time. Stand a little
back, Sir—you'll not fee them. There are
very deep, foft ſhadowings about the eyes—
you can hardly tell whether the eyes are grey
or brown ; no more you could of hers—they
looked like three-piled velvet, till they lighted
up, and then—flaſh ! 'The haſty fpark,' Sir !

The tincture of her ſkin reminds you of a
pearl and a peach ? Well, Sir, you fay true.

That little bit of hair beneath the coif, dark
in the shade, golden in the sun, is well done,
it seems to me, Sir? She was small and
compactly made, not under-sized, but of
middle height—her little bones were firmly
knit, Sir! But oh, the spirit of endurance—

We'll pass on, an' it please you. This small
closet was her cousin Britain's bed-chamber.
Darksome and somewhat straitened, but he
liked it because it opened into the Book-room.
He was hugely given to study, was Master
Britain. There's the old press he kept his
clothes in.

This is the Book-room, Sir. Disappointed
in it? May I make bold to ask what you
expected? Belike there be bigger book-rooms
at your Universities; but for a country gentleman—well, I thought it had been something
beyond common. Master Britain's hand was
familiar with those heavy volumes, Sir; but
they are spoiling for want of care—the damp
mildews them in winter, and the sun rots
them in summer, streaming in on them
through that south window with ne'er a
blind.

Mistress Anne used to be here a good deal;
poring over the books with her cousin. She

had a turn for ſtudy, Sir; it was born in her Perhaps it had been better had ſhe ne'er learnt to read. Nobody comes here now, but Maſter Nicholas Moldwarp. Who is he, do you ſay, Sir? A reverend and clerkly gentleman, though of humble deſcent, Sir. His father was houſe-ſteward to Sir William. Little Nick, as he was uſed to be called, took hugely to his book, and it came to Sir William's knowledge, and he favoured him and let him learn of his chaplain, and he was ſent to St. John's College, Cambridge.

At eighteen years of age, Sir, he was made bachelor of arts. That ſhowed good ſcholarſhip, I ſuppoſe? I remember we all thought much of it. He was elated a little, I think, by what was thought of him here at home, and he gave out that he was pretty ſure to get a Fellowſhip. But difficulties aroſe, Sir: he had become tinctured with the new opinions. Some evil in his throat, like as of the core of an apple in his wind-pipe, came on whenc'er ·he eſſayed to read aloud or ſpeak for a continuance; and this growing worſe and hindering his advancement, Sir William made him keeper of the Book-room, and ſent him abroad with Maſter Francis.

Yes, he lives ſtill, Sir. Sir Francis is dead; but Maſter Moldwarp, though his ſenior, is not. His blameleſs courſe, Sir, has conduced to long living; but he has had his ſorrows. He is now very withered, very ſhaky . . . trembling like the laſt November leaf on the bough; but his mind as clear as ever, Sir; and he ſtill hangs about the old place.

He hath a penſion of Ten Pounds by the year. That was granted to him for dedicating a Book to the King's Majeſty, which he went up and preſented to him at Greenwich. It took him a deal of pains to write, and was ſayd to be above common, Sir. What was the ſubjeƈt? Well, Sir, The Adornment of Gardens.

A trivial ſubjeƈt, ye may think, and unlikelie for a great Scholar to write upon; but I've heard him ſay there's no Subjeƈt ſo Bald and unpromiſing but a Genius may ingrayn and overlay it with choice Conceits and Claſſicalities. Maybe King Henry would have affeƈted it more, had it been touching Polemics, but that would not have been ſuch ſafe ground; for I've heard the King was apt to change his own Mind, ſo that what he prayſed to-day, he might puniſh to-morrow . . Gardening was ſafe ground, Sir.

Ye ſhould have ſeen the preſentation copy, done on vellum, with fine bordures of gold and divers colours—the gold-leaf layd on quite in plates, like as the old Monks uſed to do. Maſter Moldwarp had a gift that way, which he improved abroad.

When Queen Mary came to the Throne, he loſt his Penſion, and had to ſhift for his living an' keep cloſe to ſave his Life. We all loved him ſo well that he harboured ſafely among us, and he moſtly tables with me ſtill. But, by the bounty of our gracioufe Queen, his Penſion hath been reſtored. Happy the Land that hath a Godly Queen.

Sir, it is pouring of Rain—your goodly Apparel will be drenched, if ye eſſay to go forthe ere the Storm hath ſpent itſelf. An' you will condeſcend, Sir, to accompany me to the Steward's Room, which is nearly the only inhabited corner of the Houſe, you ſhall have, not a Manchet, but a good Barley Loaf; and three Mutton-bones boiled ; and ſhall ſee and converſe with Maſter Moldwarp, an' it like you.

Good Will! ſweet Will! hadſt thou been
in my place, thou wouldſt have made precious
Merchandize of this old Maunderer; and,
couldſt thou have ſeen the Deſerted old
Manor Houſe, all mouldering and decaying
bit by bit, and the Pleaſance ſo rankly o'ergrown, and the defaced Picture of that fair
Creature—ſcarce ſixteen at the time—and
the old tattered green Bed ſhe ſlept in, and
the old Book-room ſhe haunted—I know full
well thou wouldſt have become ſo poſſeſſed
of her preſence, as that, having brooded on
it awhile, firſt on the ſpot, and then in thy
Bank-ſide Lodging, thou wouldſt have called
her into Life agayn, in one of thoſe marvel-
louſe Creations of thine which thou art e'en
now deviſing.

Now, foraſmuch as I am at this preſent
ſhut into mine ill Lodging by ſettled Rain, I
find time to jot down all was ſay'd to me by
this grey-haired blue-coated old Serving-man,
who was not ill-pleaſed to get a Companion
and Auditor; and meſeems, in thus doing, I
may be ſupplying *you*, moſt gifted Will, with

Notes pour Servyr. Read them to the end,
then, and caſt them not incontinently into
the Wood-fire that burns on Thy Hearth e'en
in open-caſement ſeaſon, chiefly for the purpoſe, I ſuſpect, of burning waſte paper.

This old Servitor is very deaf, as well as
well ſtricken in years. You will perceive he
repeated almoſt everything I ſayd to him ; to
make ſure, as 'twere, of not miſapprehending
me. Thus I have ſent you not a Dialogue,
but Monologue.

Agayn, his ſpeech was hardlie that of a
mere Houſe Porter ; and I take it to be for
this reaſon—that he meſſes dailie with a good
Scholar whoſe converſe imparts a kind of
intelligence to his owne. Tell me your
Companions, and ſo forthe—the Proverb is
ſomething ſtale. By commerce with a
ſuperior Mind, the inferior acquires ſomething, however little, tincture from it. *Par
exemple*, I may and muſt have been ſomewhat
ſharpened at thy whetſtone, gentle Will—
albeit I am to thee as Cloth of Frieze to
Cloth of Gold.

The old Man took me through ſundrie
damp ſtone paſſages ; and whenever a door
ſhut to behind him, 'twas with a ghoſtly

clang that echoed through the emptie Houſe
Sometimes, when he fumbled at a ruſty lock,
it ſeemed me ſome conſcious Preſence breathed
a cold Breath on my Cheek or the nape of
my Neck.   Now and then, in dark corners, I
thought I heard a Sigh.

At length we reached the Houſe Steward's
Room, where, though there was little beſide
an old oaken Table, Bench, and Stool, a
decaying fire, treen platters, and a black jack
—there was more an air of human, living
comfort than in any other apartment of that
forlorn houſe.   Dozing or muſing over that
handful of red embers, with his pale, bony
hands on his knees, ſate a lean old man who
might have been your Holoſernes, returning
blink for blink with an old grey Cat.

He, looking leiſurely round, as if aſſured
of only ſeeing his old chum, opened his
eyes wide at my unexpected apparition, and
greeted me with a wiſtful ſtare.   To him
ſayd mine uſher how that I was a noble and
worthy gentleman who, for regard to *the*
Family (as though there had been but one
in the world) had ſought out that removed
place, for no other earthly reaſon than to look
at the old walls, and the portraicture of Miſ-

treſs A.ine : and that a ſquall of wind and rain having befallen, he had bidden me to his poor table to break my faſt however meanly.

Sayd Maſter Holofernes—Maſter Mold-warp, I mean—with a dignity that became him, " Sir, you are welcome. Jaſper and I commonly partake our meal head to head, as the Frenchman ſays—The advent of a third party is almoſt unexampled, and by no means unwelcome. I would we could ſhow him better entertainment."

I proteſted againſt the need or the wiſh. With a mute geſture of the hand he waved the ſubject out of ſight, and thereupon we drew round the old board with ne'er a cloth on't, and pulled at the barley loaf and black jack in right good fellowſhip. Nor was formal grace forgotten : and when the old ſtudent quenched his drought, he toaſted " To better times ; " and fetched a ſigh.

Why ſeek for better ? quod I. Sure the times are mended ſince you were a ſchoolboy.

You may ſay ſo, you may ſay ſo, quod he, ſhaking his old poll, that had a trick o' trembling already. Why, Sir, I can remember the worſt times this land ever knew—times that your nurſe may have ſcared you with ſtories of—days when the godly of this realm had trial of cruel mockings and fcourgings, of bonds and imprifonment—were tempted, were tried, were flain with the fword, were burned with fire. You have heard of it with the hearing of the ear, but mine eyes have feen it.

(Confirmed by Jafper with fomewhat between a grunt and a grone.)

Something I have heard of this, replied I, with affumed lightnefs, but what the eye does not fee, the heart does not rue.

Probatum eft, rejoined the old man, and feemed fhutting his memories up, which was not what I wanted.

If you have any exemplars to quote, fayd I, bending towards him, and fpeaking loudly and diftinctly, all I can fay is that any recollections you can unfold and will condefcend to impart, will find an apprehenfive auditor.

Sir, I am not deaf, fayd he, fomething quickly. Indeed my age is great, but my hearing is not dulled, nor my mental force abated. I think I may fay fo, Jafper? (Two nods from Jafper.) My hand, indeed, doth vibrate a little, which makes my penmanfhip falter fomewhat ; but yet I write, Sir. Yes, I write a little ftill !

I am not ignorant, ſayd I, of your pre-
tenſions as an author. (A good touch that,
Will!)

The bait took. No? ſayd he, with a curious,
pleaſed ſmile fleeting over his wizen face.
May I be ſo bold as to inquire what work of
mine you have peruſed?

Have you ever ſurpaſſed that which you
dedicated to the King?

Well—no—quod he, doubtfully. I con-
ceited you referred to that—'Tis the only
thing of mine that will live—A few brochures
that made a noiſe, Sir, at the time, have all
dropt out of ſight.

Sic tranſit gloria mundi, ſayd I appro-
priately; which was well received.

All this while the ſky had been getting
darker and darker, the atmoſphere ſtifling;
and at this moment a vivid Lightning flaſh
paſſing right between us, made us ſtart from
our ſeats, and was followed the next inſtant by
a deafening craſh of thunder. It made us
wink, I might ſay wince; for a minute we
were all dead ſilent, and then Maſter Moldwarp began, rather under his breath, to recite
the Twenty-ninth Pſalm—*Vox Domini ſuper
aquas, Deus majeſtatis intonuit: Dominus*

ſuper aquas multas.   Vox Domini in virtute :
vox Domini in magnificentia, etc.

When he got to *confringentis cedros* he
made a ſolemne pauſe ; looking at Jaſper with
meaning.   And Jaſper told me there had
indeed been a mighty Cedar overſhadowing
that unfortunate Houſe, that was ſhivered to
ſplinters by a lightning flaſh, the very day
and hour that Miſtreſs Anne ſuffered.

Methinks everything brings us round agayn
to Miſtreſs Anne, ſayd I.

Belike, belike, the old man ſayd ſoftly.   Oh,
Sir, the time cannot now be far off when I
ſhall enter the ſame Preſence where ſhe is,
whether by rough or ſmooth path.

I ſolicited him with much endeavour to tell
me all he knew or could remember of her,
from which at firſt he held back.   At length
on my vaunting ſomewhat the endowments
and acquirements of an illuſtrious, gifted
Friend of mine, (thyſelf, Will,) to whoſe wit
mine own was but as the Scabbard to the
Sword, and who now held a prominent place,
though infinitely below that he merited, in the
world's eſteem, and that he coveted and would
prize any particulars I could give him (excuſe
that flouriſh), his curioſity became awakened,

and he queſtioned me ſhrewdly reſpecting
the courſe your genius had choſen.   When I
mentioned the Stage, it was plain to ſee you
loſt ſome elevation in his opinion.

The ſock and buſkin, quod he, have been
held in reſpect from the days of Theſpis his
cart, by reaſon of great poets ſuch as Æſchylus,
Sophocles, and Euripides making their dramas
the vehicles of great and profound truths.
Yet we know too well that the exceſſive
love of the Greeks and Romans for their
Theatres, and finally their Amphitheatres, de-
moralized and debaſed them more than anything elſe.   Wherefore, Sir, I hold it a thing
to be regretted, that in theſe more inſtructed
times, wherein the pure Goſpel light ſhineth,
our court and city are alike given to the
patronage and encouragement of theſe fooliſh,
licentious toys. . . . Peradventure I am ad-
dreſſing a dramatiſt. . . . ?

(I diſclaimed the honour.)

Or a player . . . ?

(I denied the imputation.)

Nay then, I offend you not, young Sir, in
declaiming againſt one of the greateſt temp-
tations to waſte time in the metropolis, where
the language is often impure and profane,

the dreſs immodeſt, the examples enſnaring, the views of human life and character unnatural, the morality highly dangerous, the company pernicious.

I aſked whether he had lately viſited the capital.

Not for twenty years and more, he replied.

Then I aſſured him things were not as bad there as he imagined ; and it may be I coloured the picture a little too brightly. He obſerved with ſimplicity, that he was glad things had changed ſo much for the better. The old Myſteries and Moralities had been myſteries of immorality and profanity, compelling the word of God to ſupply matter for buffoons. He ſhould deem the glorious and bleſſed Reformation near perfection when comedies, maſques, and interludes were baniſhed altogether. Now we had become men, we ſhould put aſide childiſh things.

I obſerved, You include not tragedies. . . .

Ah, ſayd he, with a dolourous ſigh, we find tragedies in real life beyond any that were writ by the old Greeks.

I preſſed him more cloſely ; and at length out there came ſuch a tale of woe and ſorrow as for piteouſneſs exceeded that fabrication of thine, Will, that beguiled the time as we footed it up to London, truſting, like Dick Whittington, to find its ſtreets paved with gold.

In fine, he robbed me of ſome tears ; and old Jaſper too, waking up from a doze, and taking up the ſtory he knew by heart already, where he found us at it, was fain to bruſh his hand now and then acroſs his eyes : adding here and there ſome correlative circum-ſtance.

I made a minute or two of times and places ; obſerving which, Maſter Moldwarp ſaid 'twas pity my tablets were ſo ſmall, and half-filled already.

Then I aſked him whether he of his courteſy might not be prevailed on to vacate a certain portion of his leiſure (his life is nothing elſe) to the perpetuating with his maſterly pen the fragment of family hiſtory he had been relating to me. He ſmiled a little at the word maſterly ; ſayd his writing days were paſt . . . time had been when, an' if he would . . . but he was in the ſear and yellow leaf now . . . perhaps, if he addreſſed himſelf to it at ſome propitious ſeaſon he might jot down a thing or two, might profit

me and my gifted friend, in the way of
Chriſtian warning and example.

I ſomewhat eagerly rejoined, that if he
would furniſh the fable, we would fit the
moral ourſelves.

Fables I am too old for, ſay'd he gravely,
and ſo, I think, are you. But an' if an old
man's broken record of ſome events that will
never die out of his mind while memory laſts,
can afford you a little pleaſure, I may well
eſſay to ſupply them, for the ſake of the pleaſant hour we have had together.

I thanked him warmly and took him at his
word. Then, after ſome little arrangement
how the manuſcript ſhould be ſent me, we
parted like the beſt of friends.

Jaſper remarked that the rain had now
ceaſed ; and indeed, as I picked my way down
the ſoaked Avenue, where the old track was
ſcarce diſcernable for weeds, I obſerved with
delight that e'en the minuteſt leaf, bud, and
blade of graſs, ſparkled in the ſun as if beſet
with diamonds.

Returned to the poor Inn where I ſup, I
have cheated the elſe heavy time during a
recurrence of the ſummer ſtorm, by ſetting
down theſe particulars as a ſort of prologue

to the old-world narrative I hope ſoon to
ſend you. Till then, I lay aſide theſe leaves
and releaſe my thoughts from the Deſerted
Houſe.

POSTSCRIPTUM.

OLD FRIEND,

Years have paſſed by ſince I penned
theſe nearly forgotten pages. The old man
ſeemed to have failed of his promiſe ; but I
did him injuſtice, for his manuſcript hath juſt
come to hand, after many delays and miſ-
chances by the way. With regard to it, I
may ſay, He, being dead, yet ſpeaketh. It is
even ſo ; Maſter Moldwarp, after attaining
extreme old age, hath gone to his reſt. His
works will follow him : his good deeds to teſ-
tify in his favour ; his writings will reſolve
'emſelves to duſt like his poor body. What
need to covet this world's immortality, when
the other and better imperiſhable life is in
queſtion ? You yourſelf ſeem to feel ſomething of this, judging by the neglect to
which you have conſigned your admired

2

works, without giving them even a reviſe. This, I think, you owe the World, that will not conſent to let them die. Howbeit, if you will not hear Maſter Jonſon on this head, you are not likely to hear me.

The old man's tale is different from what I had expected—I doubt your making any uſe of it : yet, ſunning yourſelf in the pleached alleys of New Place, or ſeated within your parlour lattice, with pippins and carraways on the table, it may beguile the half-hour after dinner, when you happen to be free from the importunity of a gueſt.

NOTES POUR SERVYR

SET DOWN BY Ye UNWORTHIE PEN OF
NICHOLAS MOLDWARP, B.A.

SECTION I.

How we loſt our loved Lady.

N olde Maſs Prieſt, hight Sir Maurice, a man much beloved and of moſt ſweet conditions, was chaplain and confeſſor to the right worſhipful and my ſingular good Maſter, Sir William Aſkew of Stallingboro', Lincolnſhire, Knight. Thinking he perceived in me good Promiſe, —for, though but Houſe Steward's ſon, a love of Letters had been born in me—he induced the noble Knight firſt to put me to School, and then to ſend me to Cambridge.

As a mere Boy, I had lived at our Farm, but was continuallie at the Hall for ſomething or other, and on pleaſant footing with the young Folk. There were Mafter Francis, Mafter Edward, Mafter Roger, Miftrefs Patty, Miftrefs Anne, and, Miftrefs Joan. Sir William liked to have me about Mafter Francis (feveral years my junior), in the hope I might make him more bookifh : and oft-times we went a fifhing together. This reminds me of a little Trait that amufed me at the time, and was brought ftronglie back to me long afterwards.

I was bird-nefting one fide a Hedge, on the other fide of which Mafter Francis and little Miftrefs Anne were in the Home-clofe, gathering Crowfoot and Trefoil for their Pet Lamb. Kine were feeding in the Meadow, and prefentlie Miftrefs Anne fayth :

"Frank, the big Bull's looking at us."

"Never mind," quod he careleffie, "keep your eye on him, and he won't run at you."

But, anon, looking up himfelf, and feeing the Bull draw near, he o' fudden took Panic and fled for his Life, and vaulted over the ftyle, leaving the brave little Mayd facing the Bull as he had bidden her. I made no moe ado, but cleared the ftyle the next moment, and caught her out of danger. When I afked her "Were ye not feared?" fhe made anſwer, "A little, but Frank told me there was no Peril if I faced it." When I aſked Maſter Francis how his practice came to be ſo diverſe from his precept, he looked confuſed, but did not ſay.

I was fifteen yeares old when I entered St. John's College, Cambridge. The univerſity roll was at that time full of great Names. My tutor was Hugh Fitzherbert, Fellow of St. John's, who, with his ſworn friend Pember, deſpiſed not my youth, but incited me to preſs forward in the Race that was ſet before me. ·

By applying to my Studies with all Diligence, I took my Bachelor's Degree at the age of Eighteen, which was accounted early. I had good hope of a Fellowſhip before Twenty. But a Squinancy in my Throat left ſuch a weakneſs behind it as prevented all hope, for the time being, of my Lecturing or ſpeaking in Publique ; and this diſappointment, together with ſome Diſcountenance from Doctor Medcalfe, who held me too much led away by what was termed "the new learning," and therefore warned all the Fellows not to be ſo bold as to give me their Voyce in the Election—ſo affected my Health and diſtempered my Spirits, as that I was forced to return home to be nurſed, having been abſent from it three years. And there-after, Sir William made me keeper of his Book-room.

'Tis pity, o' my Life, when narrow Means mate wide Aſpirings. Sir William's Means were not narrow, for a Countrie Gentleman dwelling on his own Eſtate; but acquaint-ance with a too luxurious Court had greatly ſtraitened him. He had attended King Henry the Eighth to the Field of Cloth of Gold, with as faire an equipage and retinue as any Knight in Lincolnſhire could have boaſt-ed. But he paid dear for his ſhort Glorye. I need not remind ye that the nobilitie and gentry of England and France vyed with each other on that Occaſion in laviſh Ex-penſe. Many of 'em involved themſelves in great Debts, and were not able by the Penury of all theire after Lives, to repair the coſt of that vaine Splendour of ſo ſhorte Duracion.

Sir, it was thus with Sir William. When he returned to Stallingboro', all the crunty Gentry flocked about him to heare how and about it, and there was much Feaſting, much Entertayning, much Carouſing, and much

Jeſting that was not convenient. All the
while, Sir William had a Thorn in his heart
that he maſked under a ſmiling face ; and
when the Round was run, and we ſettled into
our Places agayn, he took a ſtrict account of
his Houſehold and Eſtate, to ſee how he
could retrench, and his Retinue was di-
miniſhed, and timber was cut down, and land
was ſold, and the tables were mulcted of
certayn Meates, and Scambling-days came
not onlie in Lent, and oftener than on Mon-
days and Saturdays. I uſed full oft to ſee the
Chequirroills, and I remember the Servants
were to have no Board Wages in thoſe Days,
they went about their own Buſineſſe, and
Chickens were onlie to be ſerved at Sir
William's Meſs, and Woodcocks to be bought
at a Penny a-piece at the moſt, and Sea Pies
at principall Feaſts and no other, and the
ſame with Herons and Cranes, and Pygges
not to coſt more than iv*d.* or v*d.* That was
the old Rule ; and if the Caterer raiſed the
Prices of his Stuff otherwiſe than he was
wont to do, he was to be reaſoned with upon
it. But now, ſmall Birdes were not to come
to table at all, ſave ſuch as we ſnared ourſelves, and no white Salt was to be uſed, ſave

for Sir William's Mefs, and no Lambs be bought, when dear, e'en for the firft Mefs, nor yet Stockfifh we wanted not, for its cheapnefs ; all Beer to be brewed in the Houfe, all Bread made in the Bakehoufe, all Vinaigre made of ye broken Wines ; and Leathern not Earthen Jacks ufed by the Men for drinking. In fine, I think Sir William would ha' been glad, had we been created without mouths, like the *Aftomi*, that People of whom Pliny fpeaks : not but what I hold that ftory to be Fable or Fancy, derived, maybe, from their covering the lower part of their Faces.

Now, all this fkimping proceeded from an honeft, honourable defire in Sir William, to pay his Debts and recover his Independence, wherefore we did not mind it much, at leaft I did not, though it hurt me for my Father to be fo hauled over the Coals as he often was.

This was the ftate of Houfekeeping ftill carrying on when I became one of the Houfe-hold ; but we were all mighty happy in our feverall fafhions ; for in truth, Ill-humours could fcarce abide where my Lady was, fo fweet and gracioufe was her nature. But I

noted a Penſiveneſs on her dear face it had
ne'er worn before, which I now think aroſe
from a Preſcience of her Fate. She was very
kind to me ; woulde preſcribe Honey and
Borax for my Throat, and divers Syrops and
Emollients. Some travelled Perſonage had
told her of the wondrous fair Gardens in
Italy ; and one of her Delices was to work
out her pretty fantaſies on the old Pleaſance,
wherein I oft aſſiſted her with my Mathe-
matiques in laying out Geometrical Figures.
Sometimes ſhe would ſay, "If I had your
ready Pen, Nicholas, I would work it out on
Paper."

Sir William had loved to humour her
hitherto, and had gone to much expenſe for
Lapidary-work ; but now, when ſhe wiſhed
for a Fountain, he ſayd, "In a word, my
Love, it may not be afforded." She uttered
not a word of Diſappointment, but quietlie
counter-ordered ſome adornments ſhe had
intended for her Grotto ; and I believe ſhe
bought not ſo much as a kerchief or quoiffure
from that moment, but made thoſe ſhe had
by her, ſerve.

In a little while, ſhe was ſnatched from us ;
leaving in her place a little, wawling Infant.

2*

The blow fell on us like a Thunder-clap : the cheerfulle Manſion became a Funebral Mauſoleum. The Chamber ſhe had died in was ſhuttered and locked up : that which Sir William adopted in its ſtead was the diſmalleſt in the Houſe. In place of Mirrours and pleaſant Pictures, it had a Skull and Croſſbones, a Relic or two, and a Spaniſh painting of the Martyrdom of St. Lawrence. In this Chamber Sir William long time immured himſelf, macerating his body with long faſting, breaking his reſt with untimeous vigils, ſo that he became more like a Spectre than a Man.

All this partook of a humorous Mellancholie which the good Chaplain Sir Maurice called moſt unwholeſome. The Houſe was ſo dulled by it, that Maſter Francis, now fifteen, was the leſs loath to go to Cambridge, albeit with little turn for ſtudy. His younger brothers were left pretty much to their own devices, with the Gamekeepers or in the Stables ; the little Ladies were ſecluded out of ſight in the Nurſery ; which we greatly deplored, becauſe their pretty voices, though like to pierce the Father's Heart at firſt, would have fed a ſweet Humanity, and ſoon have proven his greateſt Solace.

After fome weeks, however, Sir William took order for a better difpoficion of his Houfehold. Miftrefs Patty was fetched away by one of her Aunts, who thenceforth brought her up : and Sir William's bewidowed Sifter, Miftrefs Britain, came to rule over his houfe, bringing her onlie Son, Mafter Edmund, to take the run of the houfe with his Coufins.

And now, little pattering feet would agayn find their way into the Book-room, and when Sir William went forth to ride, his abfence might be known by the fhrieks of Laughter at being tickled and chafed about, that rang through the Houfe. I was ftudying hard at that time, maftering fundrie living Languages, but oft-times I fet my Books afide to fport with the Children and tell them ftoryes ; while Miftrefs Britain was bufy in the Store-room or Stille-room, or overfeeing the Kitchen from the little, latticed Gallery.

Shortlie thefe Joculations were held to have paffed bounds. Sir William fummoned me to him one day, and thus befpake me :—

" Nicholas, there is a way in which thou mayft make thyfelf a little lefs unprofitable to me. The children are growing miforderly, they are old enough now to apply to regular tafkes. See to it, therefore, that they henceforth come to thee for tutoring. Even Miftrefs Anne is equal to her Letters."

'Twas fourly fpoken; but never was office more readilic accepted. I fayd—

"Sir William, to perform your beheft will be the greateft of pleafure to me," and bowed lowlie before him.

"See ye fpoil them not," fayd he fternly. "You muft have a little rod."

"Very well, Sir," fayd I, knowing that an' I had fayd I trufted there would be no neede, he would have fupplyed one himfelf, and a thick one.

"I was not half whipt myfelf," added he, as I turned to go. "Had I been better corrected, as a boy, I had been a better man."

"We all need correction fometimes, Sir," fayd I mildlic:—on my life, only to fay fomething infteade of nothing.

"O indeed! and pray, what correction do *l* want?"

I ftoode abafht, and fayd, "Indeed, Sir William, I know not."

"I fhould think fo," fayd he fhortly. Then, as I quickened my pace toward the Door, he called me back, and fayd feverely—

" You do not mean to imply, I ſuppoſe, that my great and dreadful Bereavement was ſent as a Correction ?"

" No more, Sir," anſwered I deprecatinglie, " than the Tower that fell on the Galileans."

" Good ſo . . . onlie, whenever people harbour ill of me in their Thoughts, I had much rather they ſpake it out."

" Good Sir William . . . mine honoured Patron," cried I, " what call could I, your moſt unworthie Servant, poſſibly have to harbour evill Thoughts of one who has onlie accumulated Kindneſſes on me ?   I ſhould be of all Men the moſt ungratefull ! "

" Well, I think you would," ſayd he, ſoftening.   " There, go now . . . I've no more to ſay Get you gone.   And mind ! don't forget the rod ! "

I ſuppoſe this was reiterated left I ſhould go away too happy.   O how diſtempered was the poor Knight's mind ! how changed from what it was aforetime.   I found little Miſtreſs Anne in the Book-room, playing with her Dolls ; which ſhe would fain make me kiſs. Then ſhe got upon my knee, and laid her ſatin-ſoft cheek next mine.

" The idea," thought I, as I careſſed her

with delight, "of fcoring this foft fkin with ftripes!" And I recalled the Scriptural ex-preffion, "his fkin came agayn unto him, *like the fkin of a little child.*" And agayn, Ifay fayth "the Calf, and the young Lion, and the Fatling together, *and a little child fhall lead them.*" And agayn what fayd our Saviour? "Of fuch is the kingdom of Heaven."

I was a young Man then, I am an old Man now; but I hold ftill, as I ever did, that young children are better allured to Learning by Love than Beating. Obedience there muft be; that's the foundation-ftone of all; but that may be obtained by a wife Love.

Thus, I aimed to draw rather than drive my young charges to their tafkes; and did fo with faire fuccefs. The young Gentlemen, indeede, were fomewhat obftreperous; but the promife of a Story, or to help them catch a Trout, or bend their Bow, or make a Ball for 'em, ftrengthened my hold on them mightily. The Rod, indeed, was made, though never ufed; at leaft by me. It hung on the wall like a Kite on a Barn-door, till one unluckie day, when Miftrefs Anne

committed ſome childiſh Miſdemeanour.
I believe ſhe would not be waſhed. Sir
William, chancing to heare the Nurſe's
angry tone, would know what it meant.
She moſt unwiſely, made the worſt of it;
whereon he, without a word of reaſoning or
commard (the child would have minded
him, r'ly on't) and without deferring the
matter to Miſtreſs Britain, whoſe province it
properly was, ſtrides, black as night, to the
Book-room, takes down the duſty rod, and in
a little while I heard a ſhrilly wail. Ah, it
ſmote my heart! Maſter Britain, who was
conſtruing to me, ſtopped ſhort. When Sir
William went out, I ſayd to the lad, "Go
and comfort her." He brought her in, all
bedabbled with tears.

Children's woes are ſoon comforted . . .
preſently they were at play in the garden.
Sir William thought he had done well.
Perhaps he had—Eli was a good old Prieſt,
but he kept not his ſons in the right path.
But ſee here—It had been better the Rod
had never been made. For when we've
made a thing, our fingers itch to uſe it. **We
think it no good hanging by the Wall.**

SECTION II.

How we came by our new Lady.

FTER this, Miftrefs Anne was
duteous, obedient, forgiving, and
loving; but fhe had a dread of her
Father fhe knew not before. Sometimes,
though rarelie, he would carefs her, and
fhe would fweetly return his carefs; but not
as fhe would fly up to me, even till a big
girl of feven or eight; hugging and kiffing
me till I was fain to bid her defift. She
obeyed; but with a droll look; making as
though fhe were going to kifs me, and then
turning off. For fhe could be very droll
and waggifh, could Miftrefs Anne.

As for Miftrefs Patty, fhe was getting her
education in the houfehold of an honourable
Lady much at court, who had fundrie young
Gentlewomen in her Houfehold, and a
Mother of the Maids to have the overfight
of them. Mewed up they were, the moft
of their time, at their tapeftry and other

work; and full glad, for Diverſion, to get
their leſſons in Muſique and Dancing; but
it was held a ſpeciall privilege for them to
get the training, with chance of Huſbands
or Court Preferment afterwards. How ſuch
training and ſuch preferment ſometimes
anſwered, Queen Anne Boleyn and Queen
Katherine Howard perhaps might tell.

What better could be done, Sir? Now
my Lady was gone, there was a poor look-
out for the daughters at home: for Miſtreſs
Britain, great in a Sick-room or Still-room
or Wardrobe, had never trained young Gentlewomen. As for the young Gentlemen,
when their time came, they learnt for to ride
comely, run fair at the ring, ſhoot with bow
and with gun, and play at all weapons; vault
their own height, race, wreſtle, ſwim; hawk,
hunt, play at tennis and bowls; of the re-
ſpective proper Teachers; all of which took
them for the moſt part of their time, ye will
ſee, out of my ſight; or when they came in
to conſtrue a little, they would be out of
breath and in a heat, and ſmelling of the
Stable; and I grieve to ſay they learned
ſtable talk and ſtable oaths more deftly than
Latin and Greek. Maſter Edmund Britain,

indeed, was fteady to his Book, for he had
his way to make in the world and knew it.
He was a pleafant, compofed, confcientious
Lad, whofe good points were not fully efti-
mated by his coufins.

Every year I vifited Cambridge, to im
prove my parts, keep up old friendfhips and
borrow books. ·Often I was preffed to remain there and ftudy for a fellowfhip, but
the defire had ceafed within me ; I loved my
Book-room beft.   To me, in return, came
now and then fome fellow-ftudent, dufty and
foot-fore, whom, as Sir William difliked not
the reputation of a fmall Mecænas, I was
privileged to entertayn ; and thus, through
the loophole of retirement I got infight into
what was paffing in the world ; wherein
Doctor Martin Luther was beginning to
make a ftir.

In my learn'd and peacefull feclufion I alfo
had leifure to carry on lengthened correfpon-
dences with college friends on the fubjects
then ftirring men's minds ; and becaufe of
my acquirement of the German tongue
(which was more by the Eye than the Ear,
wherefore I could read it better than fpeak
it), from time to time a friend would fend me

a German treatiſe to tranſlate ; the which ſometimes brought money into my purſe, though I mainly did it for love.

Theſe works were in ſome inſtances, thoſe of Martin Luther, which I naturally peruſed with that fond attention, which truth, accompanied by novelty, uſually commands. How freſh and forcible they were, Sir ! though on what ye may pleaſe to term ſuch hacknied ſubjects. But Truth Divine can ne'er grow old ; and here were what we had been accuſ tomed to count for truths, and let paſs as ſuch, proven to be no truths at all, when ſet face to face with Scripture. The ſophiſtry of the Schools thus began to be leſs eſteemed, and Scripture itſelf, like a mighty Rock and unſhakeable, to become more and more revealed as the tide of thoſe idle waves receded from it that had vainly threatened to ſwallow it up.

Many ingenious perſons were now diligently bringing all things to the teſt of the Bible, to aſcertain whether they really had warrant therein ; and theſe ſtudents were known in the univerſities by the cognomen of *Scripturiſts*, whereof Thomas Cranmer was one.

He, then a young hufband, and the fon of a country gentleman in Nottinghamfhire, had given more evidence at firft of eminence in manly fports than in polemics. For no man could better manage a pack of hounds, or ufe the crofs-bow or long-bow with better aim. His father dying early, his mother fent him at fourteen to Cambridge, where he may be fayd to have wafted ten years in puerilities.

But after the death of his young wife, with whom he had onlie enjoyed one year's married happinefs, he, being of better mood than Sir William Afkew, did betake himfelf to profitable ftudy, inftead of to afcetic mortifycations. Whereby it came that he benefited both himfelf and others ; for he became a popular Lecturer at Magdalen College, and his lectures being chiefly directed againft the fuperftitions of the Romifh Church, caufed more and more light to pierce through the long-eftablifhed darknefs.

I need not trace here, Sir, how he proceeded, ftep by ftep, refufing any ftudent to proceed to his degree who did not prove converfant with the Scriptures. Many of 'em afterwards acknowledged their obligations to his care. Nor need I rehearfe how he came

into court-notice by a ſo-called chance acci-
dent, King Henry happening to paſs a night
at Waltham, and ſome of his retinue happening to lodge in the houſe where Cranmer was
viſiting. At ſupper, ye will recollect, the
much vext queſtion roſe, Is it lawful to marry a brother's widow? Cranmer's thought on
the ſubject, of collecting the opinions of all
the univerſities in Europe, appeared to his
companions ſo plauſible, that they reported it
to the King, who deſired to have ſpeech of
him. And thenceforth, as ye wit, he roſe
ſtep by ſtep, till he attained the higheſt eminence in the Church of this realm, to be de-
graded therefrom and receive the fiery crown
of martyrdom.

When, in conſequence of Cranmer's introduction to the King, he was ſent to Italy as
one of the three commiſſioners, ye may conceit how men's eyes were fixed on him.

Moreover, Wolſey's commanding all men to
yield up their copies of the books of "that
peſtilent heretic, Martin Luther," under pain
of being puniſhed as heretics, only increaſed
the deſire of people to read them. Well I
wot I myſelf was oft-times in jeopardy for
harbouring theſe very works, which yet were

fent to me for traduction by notable pious
fcholars at Cambridge.

And before this, many unhappy perfons
had been brought before Wareham in the
Bifhops' Courts ; fome of them for declaring
the Eucharift to be nothing but material
bread, fome for maintaining that fundry of
the feven Sacraments were neither neceffary
nor profitable, otherfome that Pilgrimages
ought not to be performed, that Images ought
not to be worfhipped, that Prayer ought not
to be addreffed to the Saints. Truly, they
were knocking away the very ground from
under us ! What did they give us in its
place ? A ftedfaft Rock, even Chrift.

When I mooted any of thefe fubjects with
Sir Maurice, he would placidly obferve that
" The Church was an anvil that had broken
many hammers." But I trow that fimilitude
originated with the other party.

When I told him of an Obfervantine Friar,
of fingular piety, who admitted he had tried
the moft rigid rules of mortification, and yet
altogether failed of obtaining peace and
affurance—

" As for affurance," quod the old Chaplain
with a fmile, " if you are on the road, fay to

Lincoln, and don't know it, ye are on the
road to Lincoln nothingthelefs. As for Peace
—fon, fon! it depends upon temperament!
Go, write your book, and adorn its margins
with goodly devices, emblazoned with divers
colours! Credit me, ye fhall get peace."

And fo away, with his fweet look and laugh;
but he did not that way fatiffy me.

One day he came in with a look of fmiling
complacence, and fayd,

"I have that to unfold which will furprife
thee."

"What is it, Father?" fayd I, expecting
fome public news, fo little had we of change
in private life.

He anfwered not till he had leifurely feated
himfelf; but then fayd, with a twinkle in his
eye—

"The Knight contemplates a fecond marriage."

"Sir William!" I exclaimed. "To whom?"

He looked amufed at my aftonifhment,
and quietly anfwered,

"Miftrefs Margery, the daughter of Sir
Robert Hildyard. I tell ye no fecret, my fon,
for he hath exprefsly defired me to reveal it to
the houfcho'd. Well, what have you to object?"

"Nothing," I replied, "only it came on me fo fudden. Nothing, if the lady be good and motherly to the children."

"Why fhould we doubt it?" fayd Sir Maurice. "She is, I am told, gracioufe and well-conditioned; comely to fee, pleafant to liften to; in footh, a lady of good favour and a faithful daughter of the Church. Well portioned moreover. What, then, lacketh?"

"What, indeed?" repeated I. "Well, I hope the houfe will be the merrier."

"And the more orderly, too," fayd Sir Maurice. "Miftrefs Britain carrieth a flack rein."

"We were all very well as we were, I think," fayd I. "Well, I wifh it may all be for the beft."

"Don't wifh it, though, in a tone as though you thought it might be all for the worft," rejoined he, fmiling.

"No, father, no."

By and by, Miftrefs Anne ran in to me, took me by the hand, looked wiftfully in my face, and fayd in a troubled voice,

"We are going to have a new Mother."

"Why not?" fayd I gently "You cannot remember the old one."

"She was not old!" was the quick reply. "She never lived to be old; and now ſhe is where ſhe will be young for ever."

"Sure, then, ſhe has the beſt of it," said I, ſtroking her head.

"Yes, but—Muſt we love this new one?"

"Certainly we muſt," ſayd I, "and revere her too."

"I did not mean you, Maſter Nicholas. I meant my brothers and ſiſters and I."

"Full ſure you muſt; and now, hear me, my little lady. This is one of the turning-points of your life."

"Turning-points? What be they, Maſter Nicholas?"

"See here now. Ye are facing the ſouthern door. We will ſuppoſe that door leads to goodneſs and happineſs. It is in your own power to go to it, and through it."

Then with my hands on her ſhoulders, I turned her ſuddenly about, and ſayd, "Now you face that north door, which only leads to a dark cloſet, where things vile and refuſe are ſhut out of ſight. We will take that to lead to wrong and to ſorrow."

"Yes, I ſee. What then?"

"All depends, ye ſee, on which way **you**

3

turn, before you ſtart on your courſe. Now,
if you, at this preſent juncture, proceed to
manifeſt ſullenneſs, ſtubbornneſs, and ill-will,
becauſe Sir William is about to do what he
is at perfect liberty to do—and which he
thinks, and we may all find, is a wiſe and good
thing—you will be making ſtrait for the dark
cloſet.   If you follow his will with ſweet affection, ſtrive to give the Lady a duteous welcome, ſtudy to love her, obey her, pleaſe her
as much as you can—you will be making for
the door that leads to flowery paths and
bright ſunſhine.”

"But what and if ſhe will not be pleaſed?”

"Not pleaſed with *you*, my Joy?   If you
try to pleaſe her, take my word ſhe will be
pleaſed—Aye, and pleaſe you too.”

"Very well, then, I will,” ſaid ſhe, fetching
a ſigh.   Then, dancing off from me,—

"See, Maſter Nicholas!   I'm going through
the door that leads to flowers and bright ſunſhine!”

"Always do ſo, ſweet Miſtreſs.”

And as ſhe opened the door, ſure enough,
the bright Sunlight poured in, and ſhe diſappeared in a flood of glory.

So the wedding took place.   Of courſe the

burthen and glory of it was at the other houſe—the houſe of the bride's father; but we came in for ſome of it too : had cakes and ale, carolling and revelling, an ox roaſted whole, ſports on the Green, and much gunpowder expended. I thought the knight's bravery ſate ſomewhat cumbrouſly on him; he was not ſo erect and ſlender-made as at the Field of Cloth of Gold. Still, he was e'en yet a fine figure of a man; of a proper height; thick without groſſneſs, his face broad, ſtern, and manly; his eyes ſhining fitfully from dark caverns; his beard with much leſs of grey than of black in it. And when ye ſaw him in his white ſatin hoſen and coat, gold ſpurs, broad gold chain, and crimſon velvet mantle upborne by the blooming lads his ſons, truly, the Bridegroom coming out of his Chamber not ill repreſented the ſun Shining forthe in his ſtrength.

So this is how we came by our new Lady. Miſtreſs Patty, too, came home for a while, and filled the houſe with laughter. Before ſhe returned, Miſtreſs Anne wondered much what ſhe would be like, and how they ſhould reſemble one another. I ſayd,

" Like the Town and Country Mouſe."

" No more than that ?" returned fhe.

I fayd, " There need not be contradictory, but may be fubcontrary oppofition."

" Oh, if you get to your categories and fyllogifms, I've done with you," fayd fhe, laughing, and running off.

Not that fhe knew a category from a fyllogifm, though I had defined 'em to her, but fhe had picked up the terms.

When the Town-moufe arrived, truly fhe did not fhame Miftrefs Anne in refpect of learning. She could fcarce write legibly, was an ill fpeller, and hefitated over a word of four fyllables. Alfo her falfe quantities were marvelloufe.

But then, as for dancing, fhe could bound and leap with the greateft agility ; knew all the new figures and fteps ; could tell of the new fafhions in drefs ; thrum a little on the Theorbo ; fing full fweetly (but the words were not pretty) ; had been to ever fo many plays and mafques, had even performed a child's part in fome of them ; could patter French ; and fay her Latin prayers, without underftanding one word, or caring to under-ftand.

For all this, I liked the Country Moufe better

SECTION III.

How Sir William put me in Charge.

EW brooms fweep clean. 'Tis a homely proverb to apply to a Lady. Ne'erthelefs, our new Lady cleaned us up to that ftate of polifh that we fhone again. Miftrefs Britain had gracefully yielded up the keys, and returned to London, though preffed to ftay: and took with her her fon Ned, whom I was full forry to part withal, the youngfter took to his ftudies fo bravelie. Great was the wail Miftrefs Anne made for him. "Oh, deareft Ned, and muft we'part?" (this in the Pleached Alley, when they wift not I was in the Arbour.) "How fhall I fare without thee? Who will correct my Sums? and help me in parfing? and tell me the conjugations?"

"Nay, coz, you muft do all that for your-felf now. 'Tis expedient I fhould not be with you always, or you would be but a left-hand glove all your life. Your wit fhall now be fet on new work." "But I've none, Ned; I don't believe I've anie at all." "Oh yes, you have; a great deal for a girl, onlie Mafter Moldwarp doefn't let you know it, for fear it fhould make you vain." "Why, whenever I tranflate fome dull epiftle into Latin, he fay ' Tully would not have done it fo.'" "No, becaufe he knows the exact word Tully would have ufed; and I'll tell you how he knows, fince I'm going away."—(Oh, the villain!) "Mafter Moldwarp takes a fhort epiftle of Tully's, fuited to your capacity,—fay, one of thofe ' to Terentia, to my deareft Tullia, and to my Son.' . . ."

"Ah, I love that," quoth Miftrefs Anne. " I fhould like you to write me juft fuch letters, Ned, when you get to London, all full of love and grief—"

"Well, perhaps I may ; only you muft not look to have much grief, Nan ; becaufe, you fee, 'tis long fince I was in London—when I was quite a Boy "—(what was he now ?)—"and there'll be many fine fights I fhall be full fain to fee—"

" What be thofe fights, Ned ? "

" Why, to fee the foldiers relieve guard, and to fee the King's Watch fet, and the

Archery Grounds, and the Playhouſe, and—
oh, I cannot tell the half."

"I like not what Patty tells of the Play-
houſes," ſays Miſtreſs Anne, "and you will
ſee Patty often, Ned, and forget me."

"But I ſwear I will not," ſays Ned.

"Oh, Ned, that's very wicked indeed!
Knoweſt thou not who has ſayd, 'Swear not
at all?'"

"But you put me beſide myſelf, Nanny.
You may count on me as your Friend as long
as ever we live; ſo don't miſdoubt me."

"Well, I will not: only I ſuppoſe you'll
have a wife, ſome day—"

"Yes, I ſuppoſe I ſhall, and then you ſhall
come and viſit us. Then you ſhall ſee all the
fights in London town. But meanwhile I
muſt read hard for a Lawyer, and keep my
Terms, and eat many dinners . . ."

"That will not be hard, if only one a day."

"No, only it will keep me on the ſpot, you
ſee; and that's why I muſt eat them."

'Twas worth a world to hear their pretty
talk, only I was glad the Boy plighted not
himſelf to have her for his Wife, but only for
his Viſitor, to ſee the fights of London town
Boy-like, he may be hoped to do much better

for himfelf than that, without confidering that Sir William would look a good deal higher than the Law-courts for his daughter.

So Mafter Edmund went; but not before I had fet him on telling his coufin, for his fake to ftick to her books—and then, maybe, he would think of her in London. After he was gone, Miftrefs Anne was very penfive for a day or fo; then cleared up, and went to her tafks with zeal. She was now very forward in her Latin, and could conftrue very prettily.

Our new Lady was of a fanguineous complexion, faire, and frefh-coloured; with golden locks like Aurora, approaching to red. Her keen, grey eye faw everything at a glance, and at laft fhe found me out in my Book-room.

"Oh, what, here you are, Mafter Nicholas! up to the eyes in dufty books. Do the worms get to them much? My father, Sir Robert, hath a copy of Gower that they have pierced right through, like as with a gimlet. Ah, here is one they have begun their work upon —faugh! how mufty it fmells. I fuppofe you have a fet time for dufting and airing them all—How often? I fhould fay once a quarter was too feldom. Are there any Italian novels here? I read a little Italian. What language

are theſe books in ? High Dutch ? Oh, I
know not one word . . . unleſs *ſaucr kraut*—
There are two words for you . . . Read me a
little, that I may hear the ſound . . . Ha ! . .
a little more, an' it pleaſe you ? That will do.
I call it not a pretty language. It pleaſes not
my ear : my ear is very delicate. I can play
the Viol-di-gamba. What books are theſe ?
Latin ? Oh, I know Latin. A little, that is."

I ventured to ſay Ladies were ſo modeſt,
they always ſayd " a little."

"But in troth, I know but little. Come,
you ſhall hear me conſtrue a ſentence or two
. . . There ! Not amiſs, was it ?" (She had
made ſome frightful miſtakes ; but what
matter ?) " You keep Nan well to her books,
I hope ? She is getting to an awkward age.
One does not want children always about,
pricking up their ears at grown-up talk. She
muſt be a good deal at her needle, and at her
book. Oh, what, you write books, I think,
Maſter Moldwarp? Some one told me ſo. Do
you get anybody to read them ? Do you get
paid anything for them? My father hath given
large ſums, ſometimes, for Dedications. There
was one in Latin . . . I forget how it began.
I think it was *Arma virumque cano* . . no,

Cedant arma . . . prettily turned. What are you at work upon now? German .again? Who wrote it? Martin Luther? O, the naughty man! His books are very unfit, you know . . . You muſt never let Miſtreſs Anne read them."

Miſtreſs Anne then coming in, my Lady called her ſweetheart and precious: then, in the next breath, " Why, child, you have been through an Hedge: what diſorder is this? your hair is the abſoluteſt maze: why is it only tied with a ribband? 'Twere beſt cut ſhort off—mine was cut ſtrait acroſs the fore-head, at your age: and I had a coif. You muſt have a ſet of little coifs too: they are decent and maidenlie."

So our pretty Miſtreſs Anne's *chioma aurata* was hidden under a little linen cap—but her beauty could not be hidden any way.

Why do I dally with theſe old, fond records? Becauſe of the troublous days coming.

Maſter Francis had returned to Cambridge. He had been ſent thither full young, but not ſo young but that he was contraĉted in mar-riage to Miſtreſs Elizabeth, ſole daughter and heireſs of Maſter William Hanſard of South Kelſey, which contraĉt he was to fulfil after that he had been three years at College and two years on the Continent of Europe.

: The proſpect of this rich match pleaſed Sir William mightily, and made him yet more content with my Lady, who had helped to promote the contract.

Next there was Maſter Edward to provide for ; but he promiſed to provide for himſelf. The toga was to give place to arms in his caſe : he was anything but bookiſh, and born to be a Soldier. A Soldier he eventually became, and a valiant one too : likewiſe a Gentleman Penſioner. He was married, in due courſe, to Miſtreſs Margaret Gibſon :— but that's told too ſoon. At the time whereof I write, he was a ſpirited Boy.

Thirdly, Maſter Roger : he had much ado to keep ahead of Miſtreſs Anne in their ſtudies ; and preſently let her overpaſs him. Nor did he trouble himſelf much to regain the loſt ground.

Now here ye ſhall ſee the perfect order and daily courſe of this honourable Family. Maſs, to begin with, at ſix o' the clock ; a certain portion of ſtudy ; then Breakfaſt ; then ſtudy again ; afterwards exerciſe, in the open air, weather permitting : ſtudy again : Dinner :

eleven o' the clock till twelve fome open-air paftime: Even-fong at three hours after noon; general talk in the hall, toward dufk, round the fire, during the fhort days. Study again Supper, fix o' the clock to feven. To bed at nine, after Complines.

Sir, we were, as times went, very happy: in a little Haven of quiet the troublous waves of the world did not reach. And yet there were troubles and difturbances but a little way off. The Cardinal's difgrace and death, the blow that was ftruck, through him, at the Clergy, the affumption of fupreme authority by the King, the imminent likelihood of an utter breach with Rome, filled men's minds and mouths and led to overt actions. Much money that was claimed by the Pope, for firft fruits, and levied on new Prelates, was withheld; and it was made law that any cenfures paffed by his Holinefs on account of it, fhould be difregarded. Then there was the matter of Queen Katherine's appeal going on: the King was cited to appear, and went not. Moreover, he privately married Miftrefs Anne Boleyn, whether his Divorce fhould be gotten or no: and an act was paffed forbidding all appeal to Rome, in matters of marriage, di-

vorce, wills, and ſundry others. And then the
King proceeded to divorce himſelf.

All this weaned the people more and more
from their reſpect for Papal authority ; and a
Biſhop preached every Sunday at Paul's Croſs,
to the effect that the Pope had no authority
beyond his own dioceſe. The King was declared ſupreme head of the Church.

That brought Sir Thomas More to the block.
A good and great man, Sir, and conſiſtent
Romaniſt. A great tide had riſen, and he
was ſwept away in it, ſtruggling againſt it to
his lateſt breath.

Nobody knowing what lengths the King
would go, everybody believed their own hopes.
Heretics for a while were not perſecuted : the
books that had ſtolen acroſs the Channel and
been tranſlated, were read and canvaſſed
everywhere. Tindal's tranſlation of the Bible
did more than all the reſt.

When Bilney was martyred, Miſtreſs Anne
came to me, looking very white. I ſayd,
" What is it, ſweet Miſtreſs ?" She ſayd,
" Maſter Kyme hath come over to play
ſhuffle-board, but chiefly, I think, to tell my
father, with gloomy joy, that Maſter Bilney is
burnt."

When I heard this, I wept, and fayd, "I knew him well at Cambridge. Alas, my brother!" She took my hand in both hers —fhe was about fourteen then—and fayd,

"Weep not, for ruth, Mafter Nicholas."

I fayd, "I weep for ruth, at his ruthlefs end. Tell me what they fayd of him—?" drying my eyes.

"That would only pain you, but I will tell you what he—Thomas Bilney, fayd. He had thefe words of the prophet Ifaiah in his mouth, 'When thou walkeft through the fire, thou fhalt not be burned.' Are they true, think ye?"

"As truth itfelf, Miftrefs."

"But *he* was burned!"

"In the vulgar, material fenfe, but what then? The fire only confumed his body as ftubble, while his Spirit foared upward like Elijah in the fiery chariot. Our Saviour fayd thefe words—'Fear not them that can deftroy the body, but afterward have no more that they can do. I will tell you whom ye fhall fear. Fear Him who, *after* that He hath killed the body, hath power to caft into hell.' That is God. Believeft thou this?"

"I cannot chooſe but believe it! though Maſter Kyme thinks he is gone to torment. He ſeems glad of it, Maſter Nicholas!—is not that bad of him? I diſlike him ſo!—"

Then ſhe preſently added, "The wind, as though in pity, blew the flames from him ſeveral times; but they only heaped the reeds and fagots the more about him, he ſometimes crying out, 'Jeſus!' at other times, 'Credo,' to the very laſt."

"Why, then, the Soul was victorious over the Body," cried I. "Heaven be praiſed for it. Depend on it, Jeſus never let him call on Him that way, without anſwering. He never does."

"Do you think you could bear to be martyred?"

"I hope I ſhall never be tried."

"I'm ſure I hope ſo too," ſayd ſhe, deeply ſighing, "for you and myſelf too. I'll tell you what I think, Maſter Nicholas! I know not that I am brave enough to bear burning, but I think I could make bold to ſay, in a great matter of right and wrong, that which ſhould procure me burning."

"May you never be tried—Come, let us read a little together." And I took up Horace, at his tenth Ode.

"One muſt take care, though," purſued ſhe, "that one's Judgment is not in fault. Elſe, one might be burnt for the ſake of a ſuppoſed Truth, which, after all, was not true."

"Juſt ſo," ſayd I, for I had no warrant to unſettle her, and had been accuſtomed, when ſhe, as a child, would aſk me this and that, as children will, to tell her, "That is too grown-up for you as yet." But this would hardly do now, for her mind was expanding every day, and ripening faſt, and ſhe could not always be evaded. Sometimes I ſayd, "Go, inquire of Sir William," or "Go, aſk Sir Maurice." "Nay, but," ſhe would anſwer, "you trow Sir William never likes or will anſwer ſuch matters. All I ſhould get would be a frown, and maybe, a puſh or a cuff. As for dear old Sir Maurice," and ſhe laughed in my face, "you know I ſhould get no anſwer from *him.*"

"Well, well then, Miſtreſs, ye muſt ſtudy logic, that by acquiring ſolid powers of reaſoning ye may be able to ſolve all hard queſtions, like Solomon himſelf."

"So I will then," ſayd ſhe, "though I ſhall never be a Solomon."

"In truth, the more we know, the more we find that we do not and cannot know."

" Then where's the good of going onward?"

" Becauſe a bleſſing commonly attends on thoſe who, by reaſon of uſe, have their ſenſes exerciſed to diſcern both good and evil."

" Is that a Scripture phraſe?"

" The latter part is."

" Show it me, that I may ſee it myſelf."

Thus we uſed to be drawn to the very verge of dangerous ground.

One day, Sir William ſummoned me.

" Moldwarp," ſayd he with ſome abruptneſs, " wouldſt thou like to make acquaintance with foreign parts?"

" Certes, I ſhould," ſayd I with a ſtart.

" But haſt thou ſufficient maſtery of continental tongues to make thy way?"

" My accent is doubtleſs defeċtive, but yet I could make myſelf underſtood—which is to ſay, in German, French, and Italian."

" That will do. You know ſomething of foreign monies?"

" I have acquainted myſelf with their comparative values."

" Know the difference between a doit and a ducat, ha!—Frank is hanging about and

doing no good. I want to fend him abroad
till he marries. He would be the better of a
companion who had at leaft a fmattering of
the fpoken tongues, and fome knowledge of
the monies. Of geography alfo, and hiftory,
and what is worth noting. You think yourfelf equal to this ? "

" You fhould hardly afk me, Sir William.
My Inclinations may prompt me to too pro-
mifing an anfwer ; but I will perform to the
boft of my Ability."

" Enough fayd. Your route is drawn out
and papers provided ; with letters commenda-
tory and bills of exchange. Keep the boy
out of mifchief and write to me once a
month. You have nothing to do but pack
up and pack off. I hope you will enjoy
yourfelves."

I was elated beyond meafure ; firft, at being
treated with fuch confidence and refponfi-
bility ; next, at the profpect of the fcenes before me. In fact I was a young man ftill;
ftaid and fimple, however, in my life and
habits ; with a natural fhrewdnefs, plentiful
inexperience, great honefty, and defire to
acquit me well of my charge.

My little pacquet was foon made up,

Miſtreſs Anne was both pleaſed and ſorry: ſhe regretted to miſs me, but rejoiced in Frank's getting my company, and counted on many ſtories of our adventures when we returned. I neglected not to take leave of my loved parents. Though my father was but Steward of the Houſe, that was an office not diſdained by many a Knight in the retinue of our great Earls. However, my father was but Houſe Steward to a Knight; but yet he had his little Farm, worth five pound a year, the tillage whereof kept half a dozen men. He had a walk for an hundred ſheep, and my mother milked a ſcore of kine. Nay, and I am proud to ſay he found the King a harneſſe, with himſelf and his horſe, until he came into an houſehold where he ſhould receive wages. That was my father's poſition—neither leſs nor more. He portioned my ſiſters with twenty nobles a-piece: and ſomething he gave to the poor. Might my father have as little call for ſhame of me, as I of my good father!

SECTION IV.

How Mafter Francis and I went over-feas.

T was in the pleafant Spring-tide
that we flarted—

> " *Whenne that April, with his fhowres fote,*
> *The breath of March hath pierced to the rote.*"

Mafter Francis mounted on a fine Bay
Horfe, myfelf on a ferviceable roadfter, a
Groome behind us with our bags : and full
cheerful we fet forth together, to fee the
World, or at leaft a new part of it. I will
not ungratefully neglect to fay that my Lady
had flarted me with four good Holland fhirts,
and Sir William had given me a compleat
Suit of new Black, Cloak and Beevor Hat
inclufive ; the fuit having been made up by
the village Taylor, who certes allowed for my
Growth, as if I had been an Urchin. Sir
William likewife gave me a Purfe containing

ten gold pieces for my ſole and ſeparate uſe ;
ſo that verily I was well found.

If my purpoſe were to cover Paper, which
it is not, I could, methinks, fill ſome Pages
pleaſantlie with what befel us on our journey
from Stallingborough to Harwich, and how
we fed, what we diſcourſed on, and what company we fell in with by the Way.

Inſtead of this, you muſt ſuppoſe us embarked on board a Dutch veſſel bound for
Fluſhing, where we landed next day at noon,
after much diſcomfiture from ſickneſs.

At that time, Maſter Francis was as hand-
ſome and engaging a Youth as you would be
likely to meet in the courſe of the longeſt
day. His raiment and equipage were point-
device, for he loved to go handſomely apparelled. We were on very pleaſing terms
together, for he was affable and I compliant ;
and, at firſt, my knowledge of the language
gave me ſo much the advantage, and his want
of it left him ſo much behindhand, that I
continually took the Lead ; but this was of
no long continuance. He ſoon picked up a
ſmattering of the Vernacular wherever we
went, and with a better accent than mine.

We proceeded to Rotterdam **by water,**

mightily pleafed with the novelty of our
mode of travelling. This city was noteworthy to me, as being the birthplace of
Erafmus ; and I was forry he was not then in
it ; but he, though alive, was then extreme
old (yet younger than I at this prefent writing), and refident at Bafle.

We vifited, in fucceffion, the Hague,
Leyden, Utrecht, Antwerp, and Bruffels,
feeing the remarkable things of each. I
would fain have tarried yet longer in every
one of them ; but Mafter Francis, with the
impatience of his age, was for hurrying onward to Paris. When we got there, we prefented ourfelves to the Englifh Ambaffador,
fent the Letters of Introduction with which
we were charged, and took up our abode at a
convenient lodging, as it was intended our
ftay fhould be of fome duration.

Here Mafter Francis, at Sir William's defire, was to play at weapons, and practife the
blow as well as the thruft, to exercife his
breath and ftrength. Alfo, he was not to let
a day pafs without an hour or two fpent in
practifing the fingle fword and dagger, and in
reading the claffiques with me. All which,
for a little time, he punctually fulfilled.

Soon, however, being preſented by our Ambaſſador to King Francis the Firſt, Queen Claude, and the Queen Mother Louiſe, he obtained the entry to ſo many houſes of the great, and formed acquaintance with ſo many young gallants, that his time was conſumed in one diverſion after another, and his ſtudies altogether neglecſted ; he excuſing himſelf to me for it by alleging that Sir William had ſent him abroad mainly to poliſh his manners and ſtudy mankind.

Study mankind indeed ! as if that were the way to do ſo ! It made me full anxious to know what Sir William would think of it ; but yet I had no certain complaint whereof to write unto him ; and when I mentioned in a general way, that Maſter Francis now found no time for ſtudies, the anſwer, which was brief and long in coming, lightly treated it, and ſayd, allowances muſt be made for the vivacity of youth. So there was an end.

Meanwhile I picked up a ſtudious acquaint-ance or two, and learnt that King Francis' lenity, or rather laxity, as touching the Sacra-mentarians (which was the name given in France to the Reformed), had till lately been ſuch, that they had begun to lift up their

heads and think their Redemption was drawing nigh.   But ſome ill-judged placards affixed
by 'em to the Gates of the Palace at Blois
(where the Court then was) ſo enraged the
King, that he hurried up to Paris, though in
depth of Winter, and got up an Expiatory
Proceſſion, in which he, Queen Claude, and
the whole Court took part ; after which, a
moſt ſtrict Search was made for Heretics,
who, after ſhort trial, were haled to the Stake
and miſerably burnt, the King himſelf looking on.

Afterwards, finding he had carried this
too far, and excited great deteſtation in Ger-
many, King Francis affected to gloſs it, and
for a while there was a lull, which was juſt
when we got there.

It ſtruck me that Paris was a ſtrangely un-
governed, mis-ordered city : I will juſt quote
a ridiculous adventure that happened to myſelf, which was not without its evil conſequents.

One night, we had been ſupping in the
ſuburbs of St. Germains, and, at Maſter
Francis' requeſt, I was returning without
him, he alleging ſome ſlight reaſon.   I was
approaching the Pont Neuf, preceded by a

boy carrying a torch, when I heard the claſh-
ing of ſwords a little in advance. This did
not deter me from going forward, though I
carried no arms, but only a ſtout ſtick ; and
anon I was accoſted by two breathleſs men
with drawn ſwords and cocked piſtols, one of
whom thruſt a paper into my hand, requeſt-
ing me civilly enough to read it. He ſayd he
had caſually picked it up, and the ſubſtance of
it had appeared ſo ſtrange that it had cauſed
him and his companion to come to blows.

I peruſed it with ſome ſurpriſe, and the
matter of it was this, That it ſhould be known
to all men by theſe Preſents, that whoſoever
ſhould paſs over that Bridge after nine o'clock
at night in the Winter, and ten in Summer,
ſhould leave his Cloak behind him, and, in
caſe of no Cloak, his Hat. While I, in
amaze, was revolving this ſtrange condition,
one of them ſayd, politely, " Sir, ye ſee we
have no choice but to relieve you of your
cloak, which of courſe you will have back
again ;—'tis a mere form "—" And your Hat
likewiſe, to be quite on the ſafe ſide," added
his companion. So without time for a word
of remonſtrance, one whipped off the one,
and the other the other, and took to their

heels round the corner ; and as for the boy
with the torch, he fled acroſs the Bridge, crying " J'ay Peur!" which, being interpreted,
is, " Oh, I'm ſo frightened!" So there had I
to grope onward in the Dark, cloakleſs, hat-
leſs, and in marvellous ill-humour : and was
ſo long on the road, that by the time I reached our Lodging, there was Maſter Francis
back before me, who roared with laughter
when he ſaw me, and aſked me how I came
to look ſo like a ſkinned Rabbit. When I
told my tale, diſcontentedly enough, he ſhook
his head upon it, and ſayd gravely, I ſeemed
to have been within an Ace of another Life ;
but yet, after that, I was plentifully laughed
at about it, both by him and his witty-pate
acquaintance. Strangely enough, the Cloak
and Hat *were* returned ; being found on the
open ſtair next morning, though ſadly be-
grimed, as though they had paſſed the night
in the Stable. I ſuppoſe the Rogues had con-
ſciences ; though how they knew my Lodging I trow not ; unleſs they followed me in
the diſtance.

Though this may appear to others a miſad-
venture of trifling import, it proved of ſerious
conſequence, by leſſening Maſter Francis'

reſpect for my ſagacity, and accuſtoming him
to a way of laughing at me whenever I oppoſed
any undeſirable inclination of his, and had the
beſt of the argument.

A wicked city is Paris. Scarce a night
paſſed without ſome ſtreet murder; and what
led to ſuch murders, but revelling and drunk-
enneſs? The wit and beauty of the women,
the courteſy of the men (though but the maſk
of ſelfiſhneſs), are moſt enſnaring to the young.
The Court was very corrupt, deſpite ſome
notable exceptions, as the Queen Conſort and
Queen Marguerite of Navarre. Were I a
father, I would ne'er ſend child of mine there.
Grant a little poliſh gained—is that an equi-
valent for the bloom bruſhed off? Ye would
not deem a coat of varniſh repaired the loſt
bloom of plum or peach.

Queen Marguerite was deemed ſpotleſs as
ſnow. She was called the Pearl of Princeſſes.
She hath ſince been the *Alma Mater* of the
French Reformation. Her little Court at
Beain was the refuge of the Calviniſts. She
wrote " Le Miroir de l'Ame Péchereſſe,"
which our Maiden Monarch hath tranſlated.
Yet e'en this Pearl of Princeſſes wrote **ſome**
very light tales.

Clement Marot—I ſaw a little of him : he hath ſince turned David's Pſeaulmes into verſe : but he was neither good nor pious then.

There, ſaw I my firſt Play : ſave thoſe, ye wit, our Scholars play at Chriſtmas, in Colleges and Villages. Maſter Francis was greatly taken with them : then, after the play, the ſupper ; much drinking, much gaming, much unreaſonable jeſting. One day I was ſent to our Ambaſſador on a meſſage, and he told me privily, we had better proceed on our journey. He ſayd, if I were gainſaid, he would bear me out in it.

So we got our paſſports ; Maſter Francis not offering that oppoſition I had looked for. Juſt before we turned our backs on Paris, he received letters from home ; and ſayd to me, with glee—

" There's like to be a double wedding when we get home. Siſter Patty is promiſed to Maſter Kyme the younger—Thomas Kyme !"

" Indeed !" cried I.   " And does ſhe like it ?"

" She likes the proſpect of being married, no doubt," returned he lightly.   " There ſeems no chance of her being Maid of Honour."

"You are pleaſed with it yourſelf?"

"How can I chooſe but be pleaſed? Kyme is not very ſociable, but he is very rich—will be, at leaſt, on his father's death. Old Kyme hath rich lands at Wrangle, Friſkney, Wainfleet, and Thorpe. At preſent, Tom Kyme hath but little. But my father hath ſuch faith in him that he is going to advance him a portion of my ſiſter's dowry."

"That is a ſingular ſtep," I obſerved.

"Singular good fortune for Kyme, I wis," replied Maſter Francis. "He will improve with it the property on which my ſiſter is hereafter to live."

"Suppoſe he ſhould die firſt, after ſpending the dowry?"

"Oh, ſuppoſe and ſuppoſe! Suppoſe the ſky ſhould fall, old croaker!—Since Robin is going home, he can carry anſwers to theſe letters."

Robin the groom, being ſick, and deadly homeſick, we were going to carry him no further: our Ambaſſador having undertaken to ſend him back to England with ſervants of his own, who were returning thither on buſineſs.

So we wrote home by Robin, and then ſet our faces toward Italy; approaching it through

Orleans, Lyons, and Marſeilles, whence we took ſhip for Genoa.

On our voyage, a wind as tempeſtuous as Euroclydon (they call it Tramontana) over-took us, and, blowing very hard from land, between the gaps of the mountains, raiſed on a ſudden ſo great a ſea, that we were almoſt abandoned to deſpair. The Pilot gave us up for loſt, and the Sailors fell to their prayers. A Prieſt on board confeſſed many of us, as in the article of death ; amongſt others, Maſter Francis, who was ſore diſtraught and in the moſt abſolute terror.

For me, though I believed my end very near, a calm poſſeſſed me I could no ways account for : it originated not in myſelf ; it could not be from beneath ; then it muſt have been from above. *Deus noſter refugiam et virtus, adjutor in tribulationibus.*

And now, when we were weary, and ſpent in pumping and baling out water, it pleaſed God of His own proper mercy to allay the Storm, and ſo we were at the Haven where we would be : noting, with rapture, the charm-ing Villas ſcattered over the Hills, and inhal-ing the odours of Orange, Citron, and Jaſmine, that were wafted off ſhore.

SECTION V.

What befel us in Foreign Parts.

E reached Genoa at a feafon of inconceivable ftir and buftle, the Harbour crowded with Galleys, for the famous Andrew Doria, Lord High Admiral of the Imperial Fleet, was about to put to fea. We had arrived in the very Nick of Time : the grandeur of the fcene was incredible ; and Mafter Francis, for all his late fears on the tempeftuous deep, could hardly be reftrained from enrolling himfelf in the forces as a Volunteer.

We landed by the Pratique houfe, where, after ftrict examination by the Sindaco, we were had to the Ducal Palace, and, our names having been taken down there, were conducted to our Inn.

Genoa could not immediately fubfide from its ferment, and it feemed the gayeft, moft enchanting place in the world. The Palaces, with their court-yards adorned with fculptures and orange-trees, were of excellent beauty ; but what delighted me beyond meafure were the Gardens, beautiful with terraces, marble ftairs, urns, fountains, and grottoes, moft delectable to behold, which I have already enlarged on in my Treatyfe On the Adornment of Gardens, dedicated to the King.

So again, at Ferrara, where I was inexpreffibly pleafed with the Gardens of the Belvedere Palace ; and, again, the Gardens of the Pitti Palace at Florence, which I have dilated on in another place. Ah, what beauties !—

At Ferrara, Sir, where Mafter Francis was courteoufly received by Duke Ercole and Duchefs Renée, we faw the famous poet Ariofto and his venerable mother, in the modeft manfion beftowed on him by the Duke.

At Arezzo, we had a glimpfe of the famous Michel Angelo Buonarroti.

O, the delight I experienced in beholding Padua ! and the bufy fcene its vaulted ftreets prefented, as ftudents from Turkey, Arabia, Perfia, and every land in Chriftendom, poured forth from fome popular Lecture. Fain would

I ave tarried long time in that learned City a d made acquaintance with ſome of its Uni-verſity Doctors ; but Maſter Francis was for preſſing forward to Venice, ſo I needs muſt yield. Hitherto we had travelled vetturino, that is on hired horſes with a Guide ; but now we embarked in a ſtout veſſel, ſailed down the Adige, into the Adriatic, and beheld the beautiful City, contemplating herſelf as in a Mirrour in the tremulous waters.

As ſoon as we landed, we were conducted to the Dogana ; after which we took up our quarters at a good Inn near the Rialto.

After ſupper, Maſter Francis propoſed our going forth in a Gondola, which pleaſed me well. Moſt delightful was it to float over the liquid ſurface of thoſe watery ſtreets of gor-geous Palaces, with their flights of ſteps, terraces, and balconies, and to catch glimpſes of fair women and ſtately cavaliers leaning over the balluſtrades, or deſcending or aſcend-ing the marble ſtairs—to ſee other Gondolas, with their high ſteel beaks, and taſſelled cur-tains, dart out from unſeen coverts and glide by as ſilently as bats ; while others gave forth ſilvery ſounds of muſic and mirth. At ſundry points, the Gondolas were ſo crowded together

that they were like to fink one another, fwaying fearfully to one fide. All the nobility
feemed out on the Canals, enjoying the pleafant frefhness of the air after a hot fummer day.

Sometimes the Gondolier ufed his oar as a
helm, and let the little veffel float idly at its
will. We lingered on the water till long after
the general concourfe had difperfed, and till
lights began to glimmer through windows,
and purple night fet in, glorified by an infinity
of ftars, and till the moon arofe and caft broad
lights and deep black fhadows. Now and then
a folitary Gondola fleeted paft like a swallow
on the wing ; and once, a large one, clofely
curtained with black, and with muffled oars,
paffed noifeleffly along in the deep fhadow ;
and our Gondolier told us, when it had paffed,
that it belonged to the Inquifition, and was
carrying forth a prifoner, or prifoners, to be
drowned in the Laguna. A forrowful death,
I thought ; and I ftrained my ears, though
vainly, to hear the fatal plafh.

At length, we bade the fellow carry us
back to the Inn : we were fome way from it ;
the Canals were now deferted.

All at once, we heard afar off, with a furprife that gave a thrill, a rich and melodious

voice chanting ſomewhat in metre, the effect of which was moſt entrancing. No ſooner did it ceaſe, than we were ſtartled by hearing our own Gondolier take up the refrain and give a replication of the ditty in a loud, harſh voice. He ceaſed; the other reſponded; then he again; and thus they alternated ſtanza after ſtanza, till the ſtrange Gondolier paſſed us like a ſhot, and we preſently heard his voice in the remote diſtance, dying into the ſilence of night. 'Twas Arioſto theſe Gondolieri were ſinging; methought that was a popularity to be proud of.

As we rounded a corner, we came on a flight of marble ſtairs, which an old and weighty gentleman, whoſe Gondola had juſt glided away, was ſlowly aſcending; when I was ware of two Miſcreants lurking behind a Pillar to waylay him. I had ſcarce pluckt Maſter Francis by the ſleeve and pointed them out, when they aſſailed the old dignitary, who uttered a loud and terrified cry of "*Al Soccórso!*"

Maſter Francis was up with him the next inſtant, his ſword whipt out; and the Ruf-fians, ſeeing they had more than they bar-gained for, ran off into the dark.

"Cheerly, cheerly, Signor!" ſays Maſter Francis. "Have they hurt you?"

"A mere prick, my brave young friend,' returns the other; and then enſewed great ſalutations and courteſies, ending in his con-ſtraining Maſter Francis to go into his Palace, which he did, after ſlightly calling to me from where he ſtood, to go back to the Inn, and bid the Gondolier return for him.

I liked not this; I liked not loſing ſight of him, nor knowing into what hands he had fallen: however, I gathered from the Gondo-lier that the Senator Cornaro (for his rank was no leſs) was of one of the nobleſt houſes in Venice; and he told me alſo that the waylay-ers were probably no mere Pilferers, but a couple of Bravoes hired by ſome Enemy to ſlay the old Man, out of ſome Spite and Revenge.

When Maſter Francis returned, which was very late, he reproved me for waiting Supper for him—ſaying he had ſupped with the Sena-tor and his fair daughter. He was in high ſpirits, for he had been made much of, on account of his ſuccour of the old Gentleman; and thenceforth he had free acceſs to **the** Palace as a cheriſhed Gueſt.

Thereafter we were much divided. He never put me forward, or made me known to Signor Cornaro ; fo that I wift not what his employments were, nor into what fort of company he had fallen. Once, when I intimated I would gladly have borne him company, he fayd flightly, " Your clothes are too fhabby,"—which hurt me, for they were always well brufhed, and by no means threadbare. And as almoft every one in Venice wore black, why, I was not fo far out of the Fafhion. Had it not been for the Tone he took over me, I fhould have been content enough to have my time at my own difpofe ; but that was not what I had been fent abroad for.

However, having remonftrated as well as I could, I did not fee what remained left undone that I could have done ; fo I made e'en the beft of it, and lookt about the place a little, and faw the Arfenal, and the Churches, and the Ducal Palace ; the Courts of Juftice, the Senate-houfe, and the Exchange ; but all with a kind of diffatiffaction.

A gentleman whom I met at the *tavola ordinaria*, helped me chiefly to the feeing of thefe, and alfo to fee fome Libraries and

book-fhops.   I was much tempted to buy a
Hebrew Pfalter, the firft that had iffued from
the prefs, as alfo an Italian tranflation of the
Bible printed at Venice in 1471, for the
curiofity and intereft of it ; but counting the
coft, found it prudent to abftain, though my
companion feemed rather forry I did not.
Afterwards I was told he was a Spy.

But before I knew that, he took me to
feveral Painters' Studios, where I picked up
fome hints of colouring; and alfo to fome
factories and curiofity-fhops.

I found Venice was a very wicked place.
I heard tales of treachery, malice, and revenge, beyond belief.   It was a noted place
for poifoning, and the inventing of the moft
cruel and fubtile inftruments of Torture.
For example : I faw a Chair fo contrived as
to catch faft any Perfon that fhould fit down
in it, by certain fprings in the back and
fides, which on fitting down fhould furprife
him by inclofing his arms and thighs, with
true Italian treachery.   Likewife I faw a
thing more fearful than cruel, which is to
fay, a goggle-eyed Satyr's Head, which by
fome contrived machinery could utter a
human voice ; a conceit that might affright

perhaps others beſide Women and Children.

I became apprehenſive that Maſter Francis was following evil courſes. In England he had been a worthy youth, though ſomewhat wilful and idle. Among the reſpectable Hollanders he maintained the good report of his family. In France, the corrupt influence of the Queen Mother Louiſe extended beyond the Court to the Capital and Country, juſt as the Circles made by a Stone caſt into the Water extend one beyond another. Hence, a Levity of Manners, a Looſeneſs of Speech, a Lightneſs of Conduct, that could not but be very bad Examples to the young.

In Italy, we found ourſelves among a more decent, decorous People, rarely endowed and moſt plauſible of Speech. But they are profound Diſſimulators: their own Hiſtory bewrays it: they e'en make it a Science. Still, they themſelves maintain that no one is ſo bad as "*L' Ingleſe Italianato*"—the Italianified Engliſhman.

Now, while I was leading an anxious, unquiet life, I received a letter from Sir William, accuſing me cf groſs miſmanage-

ment of our Expenditure, which he underftood was owing to my unacquaintance with
the Monies and Current Prices of Italy;
adding roundly that he would have no fuch
Waftry, and that if I looked not fharp, he
would prefently recal me.

This letter took me quite by Surprife, and
occafioned thoughts that were moft painful.
It was apparent that Mafter Francis had
written home to his father, without my
knowledge, things that difparaged me and
that were untrue; for the purpofe, namely,
of excufing his own profufion at my Expenfe.

I turned in my thoughts how I fhould
handfomely clear myfelf to Sir William
without inculpating his Son, but could come
to no conclufion; fo, to conftrain myfelf,
as 'twere, to a cheerfuller frame, I went
forth to the *Mercera*, a fpot where any but
the defolateft mind might furely find amufe-
ments.

For there, on either hand, you behold the
faireft Shops in the World, tapeftried, as
'twere, with Cloth of Gold and rich Damafks
hung from the firft-floor Windows, delight-
ing the Eye with every conceivable allure-
ment of Fabric and Colour: there, again, are

Perfumery-ſhops, regaling exquiſitely the Smell with odours of Roſe, Violet, Pink, and every odoriferous Flower, while the ſenſe of hearing is captivated by the warbling of numerous Nightingales in Gilded Cages hung up in the Shops ; ſo that, ſhutting your eyes, you might conceit yourſelf in ſome Woody Lane or Copſe, rather than in the midſt of a City. And no ſound of wheel or hoof ; nothing but the *ſuſurra* of innumerable Voices, the ringing of Bells, and the melody of ſtringed and wind Inſtruments.

So cheerful a ſcene might well have cheated my ſadneſs ; but it did not, for, as I entered the Mercera, I encountered Maſter Francis, walking in the too familiar Italian faſhion, with his arm about the neck of a gay young Nobleman. I ſaluted him with gravity as I paſſed : he reſponding by a ſcarce perceptible nod. Said Signor Zeno, "*Conoſce coſtui ?*" He replied with ſlightneſs, "*Io lo conoſco,*"— as if he juſt knew me by ſight and that were all.

This ſtung me, and did not the better fit me for ſhowing him his father's letter, which I did next time we met, keeping my eye on him while he read it.

He coloured high, and ſayd, with choler, "Have you nothing better to do than to ſtare? What is this Coil? You know as well as I do that we are ſhort of Money, and had beſt beware of making Miſchief between my Father and me."

I ſayd, nothing would occaſion me greater concern than to do ſo; it wounded me that he ſhould deem me capable of ſuch baſeneſs. He ſayd imperiouſly, "Peace, minion!" which was a term he certainly was no ways entitled to uſe, but he meant to hurt me, and did. I was prudent enow to take his advice, and held my peace.

But the pleaſantneſs of my life was gone, and ſo, I apprehend, was his. One Evening, at Duſk, a Maſkt Perſon ſtepped from behind a Column, and put a billet into my hand. It contained theſe words—"Your Maſter is in danger." I did not ſo much mind being held his ſervant, though I was his Governor, not he my Maſter; but I was diſquieted for his ſafety. To check him a little, I ſhowed him the billet. He treated it lightly, and ſayd, "The words of ſome jealous, meddling wo-man."

Another billet was ſhortly given me at

duſk "Since he will not be warned, he muſt abide the riſk. Mocenigo is coming home."

What had Mocenigo's coming home to do with it? Mocenigo was betrothed to Cornaro's daughter, Madonna Veronica, and was high in command in the Venetian Navy. He was now with the fleet at Cyprus. What call had Maſter Francis to make the brave man jealous, or give him reaſon for jealouſy, even by light, unmeaning gallantry to his affianced bride,—he who was himſelf contracted to Miſtreſs Beſſy, and to marry her on his return home? Up to the time of his leaving England, he had been diſtractedly fond of her, wooing her with love-tokens, love-verſes, gauds, trinkets, poſies, ſweetmeats, and what not. For a time he was always thinking of her,—up to the time, that is, of his going to the French Court, and ſunning in the ſmiles of Queen Louiſe's ladies.

Sir, ye are young: mayhap your friend is. Take warning by Maſter Francis—wear not your heart on your ſleeve, to be pluckt at by the idle, audacious hand of ſtrangers.

SECTION VI.

How we left Venice.

 HILE I was painfully muſing over this billet, Maſter Francis comes in with a rare carven Ivory Caſket ſtudded with ſmall Brilliants in his hand. I may here ſay, that throughout his travels, he had bought gauds that pleaſed his fancy for Miſtreſs Beſſy, ſome of which had already found their way to her. Setting down the Caſket on the table, he began to tear open ſundry Notes that lay thereon, piſhing, and crying with annoyance, "Bills, bills, bills!" as he threw 'em conſecutively on the table. I meanwhile eyeing the caſket (which I had already noted in a Jeweller's ſhop on the Mercera) ſayd commendingly, "A pretty toy for Miſtreſs Elizabeth." "'Tis not for Miſtreſs Elizabeth," returned he ſhortly, "and coſt more than 'twas worth. Jews have no conſciences, I think—and here are bills for

things I've paid for already . . . But oh ! Nick, what's this ?" and he turned afhy pale—" A letter from my Step-mother, fay- ing Sir William lies at point of Death, and bidding me home on the inftant." "Sir, fir," fayd I, "we cannot choofe but make our beft fpeed thither." "Not an Hour muft be loft," fayd he. "Take meafures for our immediate Journey. I will but bid adieu to a Friend, and turn my face homeward." And clapping his hand to his forehead, as if in Anguifh intolerable, he caught up the Cafket and was haftening forth, when I fayd, "Sir, you muft leave that to be packed up." "Tut, fool!" rejoined he, and rufhed away.

I was ufed now to his uncivil language, but did not like it the more. By and by he returned in ftrange commovement : a kinf- man o' Cornaro's was with him, almoft as much excited as himfelf, who hurried our Departure, obviated all Difficulties (as for Monies, Papers, &c., got us on board a Felucca), and in lefs than another hour we were ploughing the Adriatic.

Mafter Francis flung himfelf prone on the deck, with his face buried in his Mantle. I think young People have a Luxury fome·

times in immoderate Grief, and think it becomes them. Deep, exhaufting Sighs and fpafmodic Throes were heard and feen from under the Cloak ; and I thought, fure the young Gentleman grieves piteoufly for his Father ; or elfe is leaving his heart behind him—which is it, I wonder ?

I need not go over the circumftantials of our Journey, which, though tedious, was as rapid as circumftances permitted. Mafter Francis noted nothing, fcarce fpake or ate on the Road. He left everything to me ; and had I not been a better Accountant and Economift than he had reprefented me to be, it would have fared ill with us, e'en with the purfe Cornaro's kinfman put in his hand at parting.

Gladly I hailed the white cliffs of England ; gladly rode poft with him home ; our horfes in a lather. The Lincolnfhire air felt moift and raw, but it was our native air for all that : the country looked ftrangely flat and colour-lefs ; it feemed as if fomething had been cut off the horizon, to bring the cold, grey fky lower down to it. In Venice, a red rag or a broken blue jug in a window had abfolute beauty in it—here were green, fwampy tracts with fat beaſts depaſturing on them ; the vaſt, yellow Humber ; and, in the diſtance, a blue ſtrip of the German Ocean.

We gallopped as we approached Stilling-boro', and breathleſſly flung ourſelves from our horſes at the Hall door.

"Doth my Father yet live?" cries Maſter Francis.

"Yes, Sir, he's doing cheerly," ſays Robin. Oh, how thankful I felt ! Maſter Francis ſprang up the great Staircaſe, three ſtairs at a time, while I followed more ſlowly, and pauſed in the doorway. Sir William was ſitting up in his great Bed, ſwathed in Flan-nels, his Lady and Daughters beſide him, Maſter Francis with his back to me, his arms about his Father, who was embracing him with affection, but ſaying with ſome Heat,—

"Dying ? Nothing of the ſort . . . I'm a great way from Death yet, I aſſure you. You have only been recalled by a Woman's nonſenſe ; but, however, ſince you are here, 'tis well, for you have been ſpending a great deal too much Money, Frank, in your abſence."

Miſtreſs Anne here came round to me, and preſſed my great, bony hand moſt lovingly betwixt both her own. I thought her the moft beautiful Creature I had feen in my life. Sayd Sir William,—

"Oh, what, Moldwarp, you are there, are you? Your Suit of Black fomething the worfe for fervice. I believe I could write my name in the Duft on your Doublet There, go and get fomething to eat."

Miftrefs Anne foon flipped after me, and fayd, "Do not mind my Father's fpeaking fhort. We have all had a good deal to bear while he was ill. I believe Gout generally diftempers the mind as well as body. I knew not Lady Afkew had ordered you home, but perhaps he did. Frank's extravagance hath vexed them forelie. But oh, what a pleafant time you muft have had of it, dear Nicholas! I hope you have a great deal to tell!"

I fayd I had indeed feen much that was noteworthy.

"As foon, then, as thou haft had Meat and Drink, and fhaken the Duft off thyfelf, come into the Book-room and talk without ceafing."

But before I could do that, Sir Maurice would needs have me into his little veftry, and fearch and probe me moft narrowly refpecting all our doings. He ſeemed to know a great deal already, and to have been eſpying us all the while, by Deputy or Deputies, which indeed the Prieſthood may well do if they deem it worth their while, they have ſo many Eſpions. And when he had ſifted me like Wheat, he would fain know about foreign Churches, Cathedrals and convents, ſhrines and relics, different orders and fraternities, the ſtate of Religion abroad, the degree of reſpect commanded by the Prieſts, and religious goſſipry in general.

When I went to the Book-room, feeling like a Culprit, and expecting a chiding from Miſtreſs Anne, ſhe was leaning half out of the open Lattice, and on the other ſide of it was a good-looking young Man talking with her whom I did not at firſt diſcern to be Maſter Edmund Britain. He greeted me firſt, was amuſed and pleaſed at my not having known him, and ſayd,—

" Well, 'tis a compliment to my manhood." After which, he bade Miſtreſs Anne ſtand aſide, till he ſcrambled into the room, by planting his foot on a ſtrong branch of Honey-fuckle, which helped him up.

What a pleaſant talk we had ! Little

5

Miſtreſs Joan made a fourth, coming in and
ſtanding by my knee; but ſhe was not ſo
pretty as Miſtreſs Anne had been at her age.

By and by, Miſtreſs Anne excuſed herſelf,
and went up to Sir William, who exacted his
Daughters' attendance by turn; they ſtanding beſide him by the hour, till they were like
to drop; even whiles he ſlept. Directly ſhe
was gone, Maſter Britain ſayd to me, " Is not
my couſin fair?" " I am quite amazed," anſwered I, "to ſee how ſhe hath improved.
She is a wondrous fair woman." " They
count her as a child, though," he rejoined.
" She is ſnubbed and checked more than any
creature I e'er knew; and yet ſhe's not hurt-
ful, nor deſpiteful, nor unduteous in aught.
Her happieſt hours are ſpent in this room,
among your books: you will find ſhe hath fed
freelie on them." " Had I known that," ſayd
I, " I would have packed ſome in a box and
ſent them to our Farm-houſe. I knew that
no one elſe would trouble them, and did not
think ſhe would." " There is no harm in
them," ſayd he. " 'Tis hard to ſay what there's
no harm in, in theſe days," ſayd I. Then we
talked of the times, and of his Studies.

Shortlie, Maſter Francis' accounts were

overhauled, and I was called in to verify them
He met me juſt as I paſſed in to Sir William,
and whiſpered haſtily, " Say nothing about
Cornaro's Purſe." " I looked ſurpriſed, and
would have remonſtrated ; but he was gone.
I had little time to digeſt the matter, and
left it to ſettle itſelf. I would not needleſſly
bring it up ; and if I were obliged to account
for it, I would ſpeak the truth. As it happ'd,
I had no need ; Sir William never once queſtioned our having had enough reſidue to bring
us home : there was a deficit he could no
ways account for, unleſs it had been gambled
away. He queſtioned me ſtraitly if it had
gone thus. I ſayd I had never ſeen him play.
He ſuppoſed I had always been with him ?
I ſayd I had not the entry of the Senator's
houſe. He chafed, and ſayd Frank ſhould not
have gone there alone. I explained, as well
as I could, how it was. He thought upon it
with a troubled face, and ſayd,—

" Well, I ſuppoſe young Men muſt be
young Men . . . as Boys will be Boys ; and
have been, ever ſince Cain and Abel. His
wife's Fortune muſt reconcile me—and they
ſhall be married as ſoon as ſhe will name the
day. He hath expended a good deal on her

already—I fay not wafted a good deal on her becaufe it hath been favourably received by her family, and given a good impreffion of his means. Howbeit, I have no faith in that Hungarian opal being genuine."

I fayd, " Opals are fo diverfe, that I have been told the attempt to fix a price on them is idle. Each has its diftinctive beauty, altogether independent of weight."

" You are fpeaking of the real thing," fayd he impatiently, "which I am convinced this is not."

" I had not thought," I fayd, " that Art could produce fuch an exact copy. However, the Venetians are very clever, and the Jews are very cunning; and (under your favour, Sir William) the young are very guilelefs, and eafy to be impofed upon."

" I believe you have hit it now," fayd he, mollified, "and the Lad thought to pleafe me. Tufh, an Opal as big as that would be worth a King's Ranfom."

I found afterwards, Mafter Francis had little claim to guilcleffnefs in the matter; for when I told him Sir William thought the Opal not genuine, he anfwered, " Did I ever fay it was? I did **not think,** though, **he would** doubt it."

I ſhrewdly opined Maſter Francis had, after all, left Venice in debt ; which indeed was the caſe. But one coil he had got into he was not altogether blameworthy in. He had taken a fancy to ſit for his Picture to a young Venetian Artiſt, intending it for Miſ- treſs Beſſy, and had given Meſſer Antonio ſundry ſittings. Howbeit we left him and the Picture in the lurch when we came away. I had read to him ſometimes during theſe ſittings, to beguile the time, and likewiſe in the hope to profit him a little. Howbeit, I liked not the Novelle the painter would have ſupplied ; and when I read a Claſſique, Maſter Francis, after keeping quiet a little, would make ſome utterly irrelevant remark. Then we would fall into general talk, pleaſant enough, becauſe Meſſer Antonio was full of ingenuity ; and he would aſk about England, which Maſter Francis would deſcribe as the fineſt place in the world ; as indeed it is, for many things, but not in the way he intended. He would add that there were more good Patrons than good Painters, and that, if Meſſer Antonio came over here, he would ſhortly make his fortune ; which was ſpoken very much at random, though Meſſer Antonio did not know

it.   One of my fancies was whether Meſſer
Antonio might not put him to his wit's end
ſome day, by preſenting himſelf, with his
great, unpaid-for Picture, at the Gate.

Maſter Francis was very much obliged to
me for not telling about Cornaro's loan.
Where he got the Money to repay it, I know
not ; but he came to me one day to get me to
write in his name to the Senator, he not being
converſant enough with Italian ſpelling to do
it himſelf, and acquit him of the debt, at the
ſame time thanking him handſomely for the
aſſiſtance in his moment of unlooked-for
need.

After this, his thoughts turned chiefly to
his approaching wedding.   Mr. Ned Britain
went back to his Law-Courts at Term-
time ; Sir William was on his legs again,
though tottery ; and my Lady obtained from
him the object of her Deſire, which was a
Scarlet Satin Gown.

Mr. Thomas Kyme was now admitted to
formal viſits at the Hall, as Miſtreſs Patty's
declared lover ; ſhe was always demure and
ſtately at ſuch times, and ſeemed, to me, act-
ing a part.   His own demeanour was ſcarce
leſs conſtrained ; ſo there was little love loſt

between them. But how changed ſhe was from a girl! She would ſtill, when no one was by to check her, ſport and romp with her younger brothers and ſiſters, and ruſh down the ſtairs and bounce into the rooms; but it was as though ſhe were only trying to run away from herſelf. You might hear her loud laugh all over the houſe; and hear it ſtop ſhort in the midſt. Meeting her the next moment, ſhe would look as if ſhe had never laughed in her life; dreary as a cloiſtered Nun. She was grown thin and haggard. What a change from the blooming Miſtreſs Patty!

Meeting her thus in the Gallery, I would turn into the Book-room, and there find Miſtreſs Anne, pure as a pearl, beauteous as a nymph, kneeling before a great Folio, with her hands over her ears, and her eyes de-vouring the open page. I found her bent was now wholly to polemical ſtudies; ſhe was quite verſed in all the queſtions of the day. 'Twas no good now to ſhut the ſtable-door; the ſteed had found his own way out, and was paſturing at his own free will. Thoſe paſtures were green and freſh, beſide living waters.

Once, when I would gently have drawn the Bible out of her hand, fhe fmiled in my face and fayd,—

"To no ufe, Nicholas. I have it all here, and here,"—touching firft her forehead and then her heart.

The Reformation had made great ftrides during my abfence, and many were fearching the Scriptures in the fpirit of the intelligent Bereans.

Even Mafter Francis had entertained the fubject, in a fuperficial fort of way, while abroad; and while he brought home a falfe opal for his ftep-mother, a Venice-glafs for his father, a ftiletto for his brother Ned, and a carved fan for his eldeft fifter, he brought home an Italian Bible (the fame I had coveted) for his "fifter Nan."

So fhe read this unreproved, keeping it in her pouch, and drawing it out whenever fhe lifted; anfwering briefly, whenever the queftion was put, "Nan, what art about?" "Reading Italian."

I found her coufin Britain had difcourfed with her a good deal on religious matters. His own mind feemed to be in an inquiring ftate.

SECTION VII.

Of Weddings and Burials.

 MUST haften onward to Mafter Francis' Marriage, and remark by the way that his Italian flame had burnt out as fpeedily as Tow or Flax, fo evanefcent are the impreffions of many young People.

The Nuptials were folemnized with much State: I walked over to South Kelfey to wit-nefs them ; and before they took place, Maf-ter Francis went up to Court and was knight-ed by King Henry, during the feftivities in honour of Queen Anne Boleyn. This was about Whitfuntide, 1534: and ye may be fure, a good deal was thought of it at South Kelfey, as alfo at Stallingboro'.

After the wedding feftivities were ended, we fubfided into great quiet. It was then I

began to lay the foundation ftone of my
Treatyfe on the Adornment of Gardens, and
build it up day by day.   How calm and happy
an occupation it was !   I foon found I could
beft elucidate it by marginal defigns, which
indeed were not very well done, but yet there
was nobody about me that could do better, or
as well ; and as I coloured them in the Venetian ftyle (at leaft as near as I could come to
it) the effect to the eye was agreeable.   His
Honour Sir William took confiderable intereft
in this my work, would watch me at it, and
daily after dinner cry, " Well Moldwarp, how
are you getting on now ?   Let us fee,"—and
then would leifurely begin at the very beginning and turn over page after page, remark-
ing as he proceeded, without Satiety, which
was fingularly acceptable to my unworthy
felf, and proved a great fpur to the accom-
plifhment of my Tafk.   As for Miftrefs Anne,
fhe would rub my paints, wafh my brufhes,
and do anything I would let her to help me,
fo that we were very harmlefflie happy.   And
my opinion is, that whatever felf-gratulation
may attend the completion of a work, or
whatever praife from others it may elicit, the
true reward is in the production thereof.

When my poor work was completed, it was a notion of ſome of Sir William's gueſts, to whom he made me exhibit it, that the King's Grace would be pleaſed to accept the Dedication of it to himſelf ; and though I was ſomewhat in dread of ſo aſpiring a ſtep, I was urged on to it, and finally, through Sir William's abetting the ſame, it was brought to paſs. Enough of this toy ; maybe I ſhould have omitted its mention altogether ; but old age is garrulous.

Sir William having married his Son, would needs next compleat the Marriage of his eldeſt Daughter in the enſuing Autumn. Now Miſtreſs Patty having, as I have heretofore rehearſed, fallen much out of health, which at firſt no one ſeemed to notice, began to have long ſwoonings, which no one could chooſe but notice, ſince ſhe loſt or nearly loſt her ſenſes, her lips and alſo nails turned blue, her face aſhen grey and clammy. One of theſe ſwoonings occurring on a day that the Marriage had been much ſpoken of, Sir William attributed it to ſome miſliking on her part, and was offended at her indiſpoſition and would make no account of it, but begged he might hear no more of her till ſhe got

better.   Thereon, fhe no fooner came to herfelf, than Miftrefs Anne led her gently into
the open air to a bench aneath my Lattice,
and I heard her fweet, tender chiding of her
fifter, and how fhe fayd, " Dear Patty, my
Father thinks you give way too much, and
that, if you would roufe yourfelf when the
fwooning is coming on, you might keep it off
altogether."

But fhe only wept and fayd, " Chide me not,
Nan, for thou haft ever been kind to me.   I
can no more help it than I can help breathing.
I hear every word you fay, but fpeak I cannot
while that deadly ficknefs lafts, which comes
on every fifth day."

When I heard her fay that, I thought,
" Why, 'tis an ague fhe hath gotten, and of the
worft kind.   How came we never to guefs it
before ? "

So I haftened to name it to Sir William,
who at firft would not credit it ; but at length
perceiving its likelihood, he did fend for the
Court Phyfician, who came down at great
charges, and, after examination of the cafe,
pronounced it double Tertian Ague.   Thereon
Mifs Patty had to drink Mulled Wine, infufed
with certain Medicaments, but above all to be

removed, not only from the vicinage of the
Moat, which indeed was that ſeaſon full
noiſome, but leave Lincolnſhire for a while
altogether. Thus ſhe returned to her Court
friends for ſome months, and got quite well ;
ſo that it was ſettled ſhe ſhould be married in
the Spring.

That was the Spring in which the unhappy
Lady Anne Boleyn came by her violent Death
on the 19th of May, 1536 ; but that concerneth
not this preſent hiſtory.

In the early ſpring of that year, the Houſe
Porter came to me and ſayd there was an out-
landiſh Stranger at the Gate, whom no one
could underſtand. I went forth to prove him
with Languages ; and who ſhould he be but
Meſſer Antonio, the Venetian painter, who,
taking Sir Francis at his word, had found his
way over to us, expecting great patronage. I
told him Sir William was from home, and Sir
Francis married and ſettled in another neigh-
bourhood, which greatly diſguſted him ; and
he ſeeming quite at his wit's end, I bade him
come in and take ſome refreſhment. At this
juncture, Sir William luckily rode up with his
Hawk on his fiſt, and looked inquiringly at
the ſallow ſtranger. When I did him to wit

who he was, he fayd he muft by no means be caft adrift, fince his Son had invited him over; fo, to my great relief as well as that of the poor Painter, he bade me receive and entertain him till Sir Francis fhould be advifed of his coming.

When he had wafhed and fed and was refting himfelf, we had much talk of Venice the Beautiful and what was doing there, and how he came to think of journeying to us (which I eventually gathered was for ftabbing a Rival, only at firft he made as though it were folely on Sir Francis' account). He had met with ftrange Mifadventures by the way, and called Lincolnfhire "*quefta brutta pacfe.*" I do not wonder at an Italian thinking it fo.

To be fhort—he painted that goodly Picture of Miftrefs Anne, which is now, for want of care, going to ruin ; and he painted Sir William and my Lady, and then went to South Kelfey and painted Sir Francis and Dame Elizabeth Afkew. After this we loft fight of him, but I underftood that Sir Francis was fomewhat anxious to get rid of him, and fent him up to London, telling him he would be fure of patronage, which, however, he found not ; for Toto di Nanziata and Bartolomeo Penni were beforehand with him; and what became eventually of the poor fellow I do not know.

Miſtreſs Patty now returning home, Maſter Kyme would play the impatient Lover, and infiſt on her naming the day, which ſhe did, and ſhe had already brought her own conſent to it, and brought many fine things from London, including a five-pointed Head-tire for Miſtreſs Anne, who had hitherto worn but a coif. Brothers and couſins were ſummoned about us; the houſe was full of Gueſts; rebecks and recorders were tuning; rich diſhes prepared; ſumptuous clothes provided—and on one fatal day, when they were riding on the banks of the Humber and a fog came on, Miſtreſs Patty took a cold, and became ſo ill, ſhe was forced to take to her Bed, which ſhe never left alive.

I ne'er knew a man more put out by diſappointment than was Maſter Kyme. It was not Grief, ſo much as Indignation that his Will ſhould be thwarted. For a few days, it was hoped the Sickneſs would paſs off, and the Gueſts ſtayed on. But when the Shadow of Death fell on the Houſe, they all diſappeared like the Swallows, in a Day, and only

hufhed voices and muffled footfteps were
heard. When they told her fhe muft die,
fhe cried, " Oh, I cannot—oh, fave me, fave
me !"—and wept fore.   Her Father, her Step-
mother, would comfort her in vain.   The old
Chaplain effayed his beft—fhe would none of
him.   She kept crying, " Oh, leave me with
my fifter Nan ! " — which   at   laft   they
did.

How Miftrefs Anne miniftered to her
unquiet fpirit and brought peace, fhe onlie
knew.

After a long time, when Sir William and
my Lady went in to them, Miftrefs Patty was
peacefully ebbing away, Miftrefs Anne, with
her arms about her, lying by her fide, Miftrefs
Patty opened her eyes—fayd, " Kifs me,
Nan "—then fuddenly looking upward, exclaimed, " Behold where He is !" and fo
died.

It was very piteoufe, and much dwelt on in
the country.   Sir William felt it much, but
his trouble uttered not itfelf in words ; only
in fighs.   This was the firft Death-bed
Miftrefs Anne had feen ; but it did not fcare
her with any terrors.   She fhed tears of
fweet affection ; and thenceforth was habi-

tuallie grave. She would often unconſciouſly ceaſe from what ſhe was about, and ſeem looking into the unſeen World. When Maſter Edmund Britain occaſionally came down to the Hall, ſhe would affect his companie more than anie elſe; there was no levitie in their talk, nor any love-making; though I uſed to think they might be Lovers by and by. They would diſcourſe of high and holy themes, like Brother and Siſter, or very dear Friends . . . which was what they were. She would queſtion him much concerning the progreſs the Reformers were making, and of the checks they gat from the King. And thus ſhe went on to about eighteen years of age.

During theſe ſaddened and ſilent years, we had ſeen little or nothing of Mr. Thomas Kyme; but now he rode over with Sir Francis, and paid Sir William a viſit of ſome duration. What they deviſed between 'em, we only knew by the Conſequents.

After ſome reflection, when they were gone, Sir William ſent for Miſtreſs Anne. She came in to me afterwards, and ſat down and ſobbed bitterly. I aſked her what was her grief. She ſaid, "My Father ſayth I muſt marry." I ſayd, " Sure that muſt happen firſt or laſt. Who would let a fair Daughter remain ſingle all her life ? " She ſayd, " But I am quite young yet—I told him ſo. There's no hurry." I ſayd, " All young Gentlewomen ſay thoſe things." She ſayd, " I don't care what all young Gentlewomen ſay," and wept on. After a pauſe, I ſayd, " Who is the Party ? " " Did I not tell you ? " ſayd ſhe, looking up. " Who, of all others, but Maſter Kyme ? " " Maſter Kyme ! " repeated I in amaze ; and had not a word to proffer.

" You may well be ſurpriſed, Nicholas," ſayd ſhe, " but my Father declares it ſhall be, and ſoon too. Oh ! I had much rather die."

I ſayd, " We muſt not take the name of the King of Terrors in vain. Here is no queſtion of dying : it only concerns a thing you don't like—"

" And cannot do," interpoſed ſhe.

" Well, well," ſayd I, " let us ſee how things will turn."

They did not turn. Sir William would not turn : Mr. Kyme was not to be turned : more by token he had received half of Miſtreſs Patty's portion in advance, which Sir William had no mind to loſe, nor he to give up. Sure, that was the ſorrowfuleſt time the Houſe had yet known; ſorrier, by far, than Miſtreſs Patty's death, becauſe this had much bitterneſs in it. It made ill words all round. Lady Aſkew ſayd, "Sir William, I muſt ſay you too much urge your daughter." He ſayd ſternly, "In the good old times the diſobedience of children was puniſhable by death." "Good old times, quotha," muttered Maſter Roger; for which he was ſent to his chamber ſupperleſs.

Sir Francis was had over to talk with his ſiſter, becauſe that, aforetime, they had been very fond of one another. After a long talk with her in the withdrawing-room, he roſe as if to leave, but beckoned her after him; and brought her, his arm about her waiſt, into the Book-room, ſhe with her eyes ſwollen with crying. He ſayd, "By your leave, Moldwarp," and went on as if I had been a Chair or a Table. He ſayd, "Sweet Nan, come tell me, your own dear Brother, where the ſhoe pinches. Don't ſend me home with a troubled heart—have we not alway loved one another?" "Indeed we have, Frank," ſhe ſayth, crying. "Well then, what is't?

Where's the hitch? Never mind telling
me,—I won't tell again." "I can't love him,
Frank." "Nay, but why? He's a per-
ſonable Man—a right worthy Gentleman."
"I think differently. I think him harſh,
diſagreeable, and ugly." "Oh fie for ſhame!
thoſe are not words for a Lady's mouth."
"Our minds do not accord in one ſingle
point." "Tuſh!" "Tell me now, Frank,
you who have an ear for Muſique, what Concert ſhould that be in which you played one
tune on the Viol-di-Gamba, and Siſter Beſs
played another tune on the Flute?" He
laughed immoderately and ſayd, "A moſt
horrible Diſcord." "Then that's juſt the
Concert Maſter Kyme and I ſhould make
together," ſayd ſhe quickly. He laughed on,
and I thought, forced his merriment to cover
his difficulty. But ſhe ſayd, "You may laugh
an' you will; 'tis no laughing matter to me.
Tell me now, Frank, can I be compelled by
Law of the Country, to be married whether I
will or no?" He ſtood at pauſe, and ſayd,
"Why, no." "Then will I never marry
Maſter Kyme!" "I tell you what, Nan; I
ſee what it is, and will not mince it. You
love another man."

She coloured ſcarlet, and ſayd, " I don't ! "
But he ſayd, " O yes you do, and that makes
you ſo difficult." " Who, · pray ? " " *Non
importa.* No need to mention names. *You*
know, and *I* know." And he held her firm
and looked full into her eyes.

She ſayd, " I will not bear this. You may
look as you will, and think what you will,
but you are quite miſtaken." " What makes
you colour ſo, then ? Juſt look at her,
Moldwarp ! " " Sir, ſir," ſayd I, in remonſtrance.

But ſhe returned his look intrepidly, though
her cheek, brow, and neck were ſtill incarna-
.dined, and ſayd, " It is as I ſay : I tell no lie.
My heart is my own : who is there, I pray,
to give it to ? " He ſtill kept his eye on her,
and ſayd deliberately, " Edmund Britain."
" Poor dear Edmund ; muſt *he* be brought
in ? " cried ſhe, with almoſt merriment,
though her colour yet augmented. " Indeed,
I remember he uſed to call me his little wife,
but he left that off long ere he went to College ; and, I think, would not have me if I
aſked him."

Sir Francis only replied, " Nan, Nan, I
have your ſecret," and turned to the door

" Faithful friends don't betray fecrets,—fup-
pofing it one," fayd fhe quickly.   But he was
gone.

SECTION VIII.

Springes to catch a poor Bird.

FTER this, there was a dull fort of quiete in the Houfe for a few days, though I wift that Letters were privilie exchanged betwixt Sir William and his Son. On the third day, Sir Francis and his Lady rode over to Dinner, and invited Miftrefs Anne to fpend a week with them, which, confent being obtained, fhe was full faine to do, and thankful to them for afking her.

At dinner-time, Sir William looking toward his fon, fayd in a loud, clear voice, " I fuppofe you have heard of this projected Marriage of Edmund Britain's ? "

" No, indeed," returns Sir Francis ; " what, is it a fettled thing, then ? I had not fuppofed anything ferious in that quarter. What, hath the Lady money ?"

"Not much of that, I believe," fayd Sir William, flightly; and began to fpeak of a different matter. I ftole a look at Miftrefs Anne, from where I fate at the Side-table, and noted her eye-lids tremble a little, which was all the emotion fhe fhowed.

Mafter Kyme came not near us while fhe was away, and I heard he abftained equally from going to South Kelfey.

I was only a byftander; had neither right nor difpofition to interfere in the Game; neverthelefs I had my own proper thoughts and notions; and one of them was that this ftory of Mafter Britain's engagement was a fabrication; but the fcene was fufficiently well enacted to have the force of truth to a guilelefs young mind.

Have you feen Kelfey Hall, Sir? It is a moated Manfion, added to at different periods, which gives it an irregularity that to my eye is by no means unpleafing. It hath a small Court in front, furrounded by a wall with octangular turrets at each corner, and a hand-fome Gate-way in the middle. On one fide the Entrance Porch, the Mullioned Windows have five lights; on the other side, only four. There are little, ſtepped Gables over the Dormer Windows.

Miſtreſs Anne had been ſo little from home, and Sir Francis and his Lady, being young and fond of pleaſure, kept ſuch different State from Sir William, that ſhe enjoyed her ſojourn with them exceedingly. They rode, they hawked, they played with Bows and Arrows, they ſang Madrigals and played on ſtringed and wind Inſtruments, and made her time paſs as pleaſantlie as they could; giving her to underſtand by the way, that all theſe Delices would be at her command when ſhe was wedded to Maſter Kyme. Sure 'twas ingeniouſly done.

Then, when ſhe came back, Maſter Kyme rode over and brought her a rare jewel; an Emerald, with three pear-ſhaped pendants; but ſhe contemned it. He told her how much it had coſt him, and ſayd the jewel was without flaw. Then, ſayd ſhe, "That's a great deal to ſay of an Emerald, and more than can be honeſtly ſayd of any living creature; leaſt of all, of me."

"I wiſt not you had any flaw," quod he. "O yes, Sir; a very unyielding Temper"

6

"Since you trow that to be a flaw, which in footh it is," returns he, "no doubt you will ftrive for grace to mend it." "In reafonable things, but not unreafonable." "How mean you by that?" fayd he. "I mean that there are things in which others would fometimes have me yield, that they deem reafonable, but I, unreafonable." "Oh, Miftrefs Anne, there is a certain guide for that. Ye fhould abide by the judgment of your Elders." "How if they are not my Betters?" "That query favoureth not of a humble mind." "How if my Elders are at iffue between themfelves? But there! I'm tired of it!" fayd fhe, flinging away a Carnation fhe had been pulling to pieces.

Mafter Kyme looked at her from under his thick, black brows, as though he hoped to make her fing another Song, another Day. But fhe faw him not, for her face was turned afide, and pouting. She had a weary time of it, day by day: all pleafant Talk was chafed away by Altercation. One day, when fhe was leaving the room in a huff, fhe ran againft fome one in the Doorway and fayd, "Oh, Edmund, is it thou?" and began to cry. He fayd, "Why, Nan, what's the matter? You uſed to be all Smiles and no Tears." " 'Tis juſt the other way now then," ſayd ſhe, " for I am badgered from morn till night." " By whom ?" ſayd he, taking her by the hand and drawing her to a chair, and then ſitting over againſt her on a Stool. She hung her head and ſayd, " By my Father moſtly." " I ſup-poſe," ſayth he, " you know the firſt command-ment with promiſe ?" " You think to ſtop my mouth with that," ſayth ſhe, ſofter, and looking down. " Dear Nan," he returns very kindly, " you accept the whole canon of Scrip-ture, do you not ?" " Why, of courſe I do." " You deem it a great and glorious thing that Cranmer has done, to ſet up a copy of Cover-dale's Bible in the choir of every Church, for public uſe ?" " Indeed I do," ſhe cries, her bright eyes raiſed and beaming. " You are ready to abide by it to the death." " Aye, I hope I am, God being my Helper." " Now ſee how witleſs a thing it is, Nan, to be willing to die for it, and not to live by it." " How mean you ?" ſayd ſhe, regarding him wiſtfully. " I know not any warrant we have," he pur-ſued, " for obeying one part of Scripture and not another : onlie picking out our favourite texts in it. The wickedeſt ſinner that ever lived might even his conduct by it that way. He that fayd Thou fhalt not kill, said Thou fhalt not fteal : now, if thou kill not, yet if thou fteal, thou haft broken the Law." "Of courfe; that's the fubftance of St. Paul's argument," fayth fhe. "We are finners all." "He that fayd Thou fhalt not fteal, fayd alfo Honour thy Father and thy Mother," continued he. "Now, if thou fteal not, yet if thou difhonoureft thy Father and Mother, thou tranfgreffeft the Law." "To difallow is not to difhonour," fayd fhe, looking troubled. "Tut! what is to difallow but to difhonour? We difhonour thofe we difobey and contravert." "I fee they have had you here on purpofe to put me down with your Subtileties," fayth fhe, beginning to weep. "On my Honour no, Nan. I came down of my own Accord, and on no Invitation." It was eafy to fee what great Relief fhe received on hearing this.

"O, Ned," fayth fhe, "you joy my heart; and fince I think you the beft friend I have, advife me, I befeech you, in this fore ftrait." "Right willingly, and without Fee," quoth he playfully. "Show me what the ftrait is." "Sure you know the difficulty I am now in ?" ſhe ſayth. But he looked all abroad, though I trow he knew it well enough in his heart. He would compel her to ſpeak, which ſhe did faltering, and plucking at her Apron.

"Why, about Maſter Kyme." "What about Maſter Kyme ?" "You know he was to have had Patty." "I know he was to have had Patty." "Patty died." "I know that too." "Is that any reaſon he ſhould have *me ?*"

"That depends," ſayd he, with a pleaſant ſmile, and ſhifting his poſture. "Is there any reaſon he ſhould not ?" "Yes, if there's not mutual Liking." "I conclude he likes you." "But I know I don't like him."

"Your objections, your objections," ſayd he, flicking his hand with his glove.

"Oh, I can't count them all, they're ſo many ; I like him in nothing—diſlike him in everything."

"If you were my ſiſter, Nan, I might aſk . . . do you like any one better ?"

"All the world ! every one !" ſayd ſhe briſkly, which took him ſo by ſurpriſe he could not help laughing.

"Well," ſayd he, "I don't ſee my way out of

this—." "How can you wonder that I don't?"
"How, indeed?" repeated he, gravely, and
regarding her with attention. "You are but
young yet, and know not that Life is full of
ſorrow."

"O but I do," returns ſhe, weeping. "Have
not I loſt Patty?"

"Aye," ſayd he, "and I loſt a dear Friend
no great while back. It made me ſo ſick at
heart that I came to this concluſion . . .
There's no good or Stay in this Life at all,
but only to do one's Duty in it. But you
cannot underſtand or feel this."

"Indeed but I can, though," quoth ſhe.

"There's no good nor Stay in this Life,
ſave to do one's Duty in it," repeated he after
pauſing. "And this Life, how ſhort! a mere
Breath—a Bubble. It is the prelude to a
Life that ſhall never end. How mad, then,
to ſet the Pleaſure of this little Life before its
Duty!"

"I don't want to do that," ſayd ſhe, humblie.

"I know you don't."

"But I want to know what my Duty is."

"If I ſhow it you, will you engage to perform it? Otherwiſe I may ſpare myſelf the
trouble."

" Well, then,—I will," ſayd ſhe, heſitating.

" You will!"

" Yes, I will."

He took her hand for a moment.

" Duty very often comes in the very ſhape we do not wiſh. The old Chineſe Philoſopher ſayd, that when he was undecided which was the beſt between two courſes, he generally found it ſafeſt to take the moſt Untempting. Every thinking Perſon knows (only the general don't think) that there are two great Antagoniſts engaged in conſtant Warfare—the World, and Heavenly Wiſdom. Now, there is ſo much that is dear to us, on the ſide of the World! And Satan, like a cunning General, puts the very deareſt thing we have, which he holds as Hoſtage, in the front Rank of his forces !—thinking we will not ſtir againſt it. Do you ſee?"

" Yes, Ned," with a deep ſigh. I was ſure how the matter would end after this.

" Well," ſayth ſhe, after long thinking, " if I muſt, I muſt—"

" That's my good Nan!"

" And as Queen Eſther ſayd, ' If I die, I die.' "

" Die! We fhall all die ; but none the fooner, all the fweeter, for being in the path of Duty."

" You are quite fure, Ned, it *is* my duty to marry him whom I do not love ? Once prove it, and . . ."

" Cafes like thefe go not by logical proof. Our likes and diflikes fhift like the clouds. Refolve to be a good wife unto him ; you'll learn to love him !"

" Is that the way you would like *your* wife to learn to love you, coufin ?"

He did not anfwer this, but went on, " Receive his overtures of affection plea-fantlie, graciouflie ; what begins in Duty cannot but end in Happinefs."

" Well, I'll try," fayd fhe, with yet another figh.

" And if you do, Nan, it cannot but be a well-afforted Marriage."

" Oh, by the way, coufin," raifing her fweet eyes with a fmile in them to his, " I offer you my good wifhes on your own ap-proaching Marriage."

" Mine ? " fayd he, changing countenance ; " I'm not going to be married ! Who could have told you fo ? "

" My father."

His eyelids gave an involuntary quiver. " Ah, my Uncle laboured under a Miſtake," ſayd he quietly. " Next time we are alone together, he ſhall have it explained. Come, ſhall we go and ſeek him ? "

She was very pale ; her eyes full of tears. But ſhe put her hand in his, and ſayd, " Yes ; and mind you keep me up to the mark."

" No doubt of it," he replied ; " and, Nan, one word in your ear : give yourſelf much unto Prayer."

" Ah, I do that alreadie ! Where, elſe, were I ? "

After that, they paſſed out together ; and I felt abſolutely convinced ſhe was being led to Suffering and Sorrow.

Sir William was infinitely pleaſed at her yielding all he wanted without more ado : and careſſed her now and then, which, I think, went further with her than all his arguments and upbraidings. Maſter Kyme, too, ſhowed his beſt ſide outward, ſo that the path to her Fate was ſmoothed as much as might be. They took long Rides together ; ſhe loved galloping, and would return all fluſhed and panting. As for her Wedding

6*

Garments, perhaps never Bride took lefs intereft in them. She fayd, "I wifh all the feafting were over. When we are left alone, Mafter Kyme will doubtlefs go out hunting, and looking after his eftate. I fhall fit within and make clothes and flops for poor Folk, and read a great deal."

"And write, perhaps," said I.

"What, a book, Nicholas? What a bright thought! Why fhould I not, as well as Marguerite de Valois?"

"Or a deal better?" sayd I, playing on the word.

In fact, fhe had a pretty turn for poetry; as alfo for mufique. I doubt if Queen Anne Boleyn, or Lord Percy, or Lord Surrey, could make better verfes, or set them to prettier Tunes. Happy they who have fuch refources, not for the praife they get, but for the folace and refuge they afford, in **many elfe** fad or idle Hours.

SECTION IX.

How the poor Bird fled from its Cage to its Neſt.

SO ſhe was married—the pale, beauti-ful bride ! I think onҽ of her pureſt pleaſures was giving me a complete new ſuit, of excellent broad-cloth, and pinning a white knot on it herſelf. As ſhe left the Book-room, ſhe looked around it, ſaying, "How many happy hours have I paſſed here !—"

When the laſt ſummer ſunbeam ſhines on us, we ſhould be very ſad, did we know 'twas our laſt. I think my laſt ſummer ſunbeam was o'erclouded when ſhe left the Houſe ; but a not unpleaſing grey, dim twilight, gradually ſtole on, that was not for ſome time deepened into gloom.

My niece Lettice, a buxom, black-eyed

lafs, was promoted to be her woman : a great honour for Lettice, Sir, and one that fhe did not abufe. When fhe came over to Stalling-boro' for her holidays (her Lady always gave her one a quarter), fhe always brought me her Lady's kind regards, and often fome little token, of fruit, or flowers, or a book, or, may-be, a kerchief hemmed by herfelf.   Thus I learnt of Lettice how fhe fared.

Mafter Edmund Britain looked over the Marriage Settlements.   There was a fmall property devifed to her from her Mother, which he fayd fhould be fettled on her for her fole and feparate ufe ; and he carried the point too ; Mafter Kyme could not for fhame gainfay it, having alreadie had the ufe of half her portion and now getting the other half ; but he fayd, Wives fhould not be inde-pendent of their Husbands.   She was not, Sir !   He took care of that, and gave her the lefs Pin-money, and at length none.   I believe their firft variance was about her little Pittance, when Quarter-day came round and fhe gat it not.   She had a Girl's pleafure in the independent ufe, for the firft time, of a little Money ; and wanted it not for Vanities, poor young Lady, but for the Poor, and for

Books. She ſayd, half between jeſt and earneſt, that if he did not pay it her, ſhe would tell her Father; ſo then he let her have, what ought never to have paſſed through his hands. But, you ſee, ſhe had unbuſineſs-like Truſtees; at leaſt one was,—the other was Maſter Britain.

Sir William having carried his point with his Daughter, had now nothing to do, one would ſuppoſe, but enjoy having his own way: but he grew exceeding captious and quarrelous; ſo that it was next to impoſſible to pleaſe him. The only company he now ſeemed truly to care for, was that of Sir Francis, who, how-ever, came not over to him ſo often as he would have ſeen him; nor remained ſo long; and this was a fertile ſource of complaint. His ſecond ſon, Maſter Edward, was now of the houſehold of Archbiſhop Cranmer; who, on his appointment, wrote of him that the young man was of a very gentil nature, right forward and of good activity. Maſter Roger was keeping his terms at Oxford.

My good Parents had long gone to their reſt; my Brother held the little farm, which now depended only on one Life; my ſiſters were married to honeſt Yeomen and had

grownup Children. At times we heard the
news; oft-times none reached us till it was
ſtale: the winter was long and drearie, and
Miſtreſs Anne was unable to come over to us.
When I hearde ſhe had a little Daughter I
rejoiced that ſhe had ſo pure a ſource of
Pleaſure vouchſafed, and prayed the little
Youngling might prove an Epitome of her-
ſelf; but Sir William was diſappointed of
her not bearing a man-child, and Maſter
Kyme was out of humour at not getting an
Heir.

I wearied for a ſight of her dear Face, but
on how ſad an occaſion did ſhe viſit us. Sir
William had an acceſs of Gout in the ſtomach,
which cauſed all his Children to be ſummoned about him by Expreſs; but the more
diſtant ones arrived not in time to ſee him
alive. Maſter Kyme was from home, but
Miſtreſs Anne came over as faſt as a ſtrong
high trotting horſe could carry her (it being
two days' journey); the Nurſe, riding Pillion,
following her with the infant. To ſee her
hang over Sir William, and tend him with
the utmoſt duteouſneſs, ye might have thought
he had been the kindeſt Father ever was;
but he made little account of her, and only

chafed becauſe Sir Francis came not on the
inſtant. At length, with his wife, eldeſt ſon,
and two daughters about him, he made an
end, deriving but little cómfort, it ſeemed to
me, from the ceremonial obſervances of
religion that yet were duly and reverentlie
performed. After extreme unɛtion, he fell
into lethargy, and ſo ſhortly departed.

Miſtreſs Anne, full of tears, was faine to
remain in the Houſe till after the Funeral :—
ye have ſeene the green Bed, ſir, in the
chamber ſhe lay in. As ſoon as the obſe-
quies were concluded, (which were celebrated
at Midnight, a large body of the country
Gentry attending to do him the last honours,)
Maſter Kyme took wife and child with him ;
the young gentlemen diſperſed, and the bewidowed Dame and youngeſt Daughter, remained bereft and lonely till Affairs were
ſettled and ſhe put in receipt of her jointure,
which is to ſay at the expiry of ſix months.
Many Servants were diſmiſſed, the remainder
put on board wages, the greater part of the
Houſe ſhut up, and wearing apparel packed
ready for a viſit to my Lady's kinſfolk. Miſtreſs Joan, though of tender years, had
already, by Sir William's arrangements, been

deftined for the wife of Sir George St
Paul of Snarford; and fhe vifited among
his family and hers, till the Wedding took
place; never fetting foot in Stallingboro'
again.

Thus the place was left to enjoy its Sab-
baths; and I wot I fhould have beene caft
forth with the reft, but that the Manfion
was left in charge of an old fervant or two,
and my Lady thought I might as well ftay
on, and keep them to their pofts. I now
had great leifure for Study, which affuredly I
did not neglect. Now and then I hoed and
raked the Flower-beds a little, and did a
little pruning, for it feemed a fhame the
Pleafance fhould be let grow weedy and feedy
by one who had writ on the Adornment of
Gardens. Howbeit, there was work, not for
one man but half a dozen.

One day after weeding a little, I fat down
on the heavy ftone Roller to recover my
breath, when I faw my niece Lettice coming
up the turfen alley. Time had fleeted on fo
unmarked, that I was aftonied when fhe
told me Miftrefs Anne had borne another
infant.

"And," fayth fhe, "'tis another girl, as

ill luck will have it, which makes Maſter Kyme downright ſavage."

"How can he be ſo un-Chriſtian?" quod I, "when the Lord hath added another little Olive-branch to his table? Children are a heritage from the Lord."

"Aye; but he doth not count it ſo," ſayd Lettice. "Oh, it is fearful to hear how he upbraids her—not for this, in ſo many words, but for all ſhe does and ſays, and mainly for what he calls her Goſpelling."

"Aye, aye?" ſayd I, anxiouſly.

"In faith, the ſweet Lady hath no com-fort but in her infants, and her Bible," ſayth Lettice. "When they were firſt married, I know not what ſpirit of wiſdom and ſilence poſſeſſed my dear Miſtreſs, but ſhe habitual-lie kept her tongue within her teeth, only truſting herſelf to utter phraſes abſolutely needful and harmleſs. Maſter Kyme was well pleaſed with this retention of ſpeech. The firſt time ſhe brake through it was, as I told you, when he kept back her Money and ſhe threatened to tell her Father. I know not what courſes he took with her, when by themſelves, to cow and leſſon her; but when I next went in to her, ſhe was in a violent fit of trembling, like as Miftrefs Patty fhook in the double tertian. But fhe had carried her point; and after that fhe feemed defirous by the utmoft fweetnefs and ftudy of his wifhes, to make him forget fhe had ever gainfaid him. This he'd on till after Sir William's death. Mafter Kyme, who had, I believe, never forgiven her firft felf-affertion, now thought he would make her find fhe had no appeal. He abided his time; fhe meanwhile, unfufpecting coming evil, and incited to good fpirits by her dear little infant, would fing and laugh to it, and talk freely out of her heart's fulinefs to all about her. Thus her tongue became unlocked: fhe was as free of fpeech as though there was no one to be afraid of; and would bid us, like the good Miftrefs fhe is, be faithful in bufinefs, fervent in fpirit, ferving the Lord —not with eye-fervice, as men-pleafers, or women-pleafers either. Alfo at dinner time, fhe would from time to time fpeak her mind, in converfe with guefts; Mafter Kyme eyeing her all the time with filent feverity: yet abftaining from checking her, becaufe the Duchefs of Suffolk had fhown her favour."

" That was very good of her noble Grace,"
ſayd I, "ſo to ſtrengthen the unprotećted.
How did matters go after that ?"

" Quarter day came round and paſſed,"
ſayd Lettice, "and my Miſtreſs, who had
promiſed help to a poor Widow, at length
ſayd 'Good huſband, you have forgotten my
money.' 'I have none about me,' he anſwered ſlightly. I believe ſhe did this two
or three times without getting any more
ſatiſſaćtion. At length ſhe ſayd, but not
unkindly, 'Well, I wiſh Couſin Britain had
taken order to pay my money direćt to myſelf. I think I'll aſk him.' 'Why are you
always harping on Money?' quod he, very
ſharply. 'Becauſe I want it very badly, my
dear.' 'Have you not everything found?'
''Tis not for myſelf, but Widow Green, who
hath loſt her Cow.' 'Oh, there then ; there's
ſomething towards it'—giving her a little
looſe ſilver : which was not the ſame thing,
you know, Nunks."

" Not at all," ſayd I. "I'm ſorry they
had words. Widow Green would rather have
ſhifted without the money than gotten it at
ſuch coſt."

" But 'twas her own, you know," perſiſted

Lettice, "and I muſt ſay I think her right
No more was then ſayd; but next morning
my Miſtreſs could nowhere find her Bible.
We hunted high and low for it in vain; it
could not be found. At length ſhe ſayd to
Maſter Kyme, 'Such a ſtrange thing hath
befallen: my Bible is gone.' 'O, I have
it,' ſayd he coolly, 'you are not to have
it again.' 'Not have it?' repeated ſhe,
colouring violently, 'It is mine.' He anſwered, 'What's yours is mine, and what's
mine's my own.' Tears ſtarted into her
eyes, and ſhe ſayd, 'This is too cruel a jeſt.
Forſooth and forſooth ye muſt let me have
it.' 'Not I,' anſwered he roughly. 'It is
no jeſt, as ye ſhall find. I deſire that from
this time forth thou tamper not with the
religion of my houſehold. If thou doſt so,
after this injunction, I ſhall take such order of
thee, Madam, as . . . .' And ſo away, only
finiſhing his ſentence by a terrible look.
She, ready to faint, could not proffer a word;
and up to this time, hath not again provoked
him to anger. Meanwhile ſhe uſes a little
Italian Teſtament."

"Which Sir Francis brought her from
Italy," ſayd I; "I know it well."

" But it will ſoon be taken from her," ſayd Lettice, "for Maſter Kyme's Confeſſor is a moſt tyrannous Prieſt, and ruleth everything in the houſe."

After ſome further talk, ſhe left me, to ſee her father and mother, and I remained in a painful muſe on this family ſtory, till driven indoors by a ſmart rain.

The weather broke up, about this time, and ſet in very wet. I was uſed to ſleep in what went by the name of the Prieſt's Chamber, over the Gateway, which had aforetime been occupied by good old Sir Maurice till his death. I loved the little cell for his ſake : it had no Fireplace, and was draughty enough, ſet up on high and expoſed to the wind all round ; but that ſeldom hindered me of ſleep.

But one night, when the wind blew in guſts and the rain pattered againſt the Lattice, I was rouſed from ſleep by what ſeemed Voices borne on the Blaſt, and I lay thinking of the poor Outcaſts who might, e'en on ſuch a night, be croſſing dank Moors or cowering 'neath Hedges. The rattle, as of a Pebble caſt againſt the Caſement, made me riſe up and look about me. I diſtinctly heard a Woman's voice at the Gate below, calling "Uncle! uncle!" I opened the caſement in great fear, and called, "Who's there?"

"'Tis I, uncle," cried Lettice, "with Miſtreſs Anne and the two babes. Oh, haſte and let us in, for we are drenched to the ſkin, and ready to drop."

"Alas for ruth!" ejaculated I. "Tarry but a moment; I'll come quickly." And haſtily dreſſing, I went down and let her in, greeting her with "Poor soul! poor soul!"

There was hardly any light, for black clouds were faſt drifting over the moon, but a pale ray for a moment ſhowed me indiſtinctly a cowering figure wrapped in ſomething whitiſh, like ſheet or blanket, and cloſely claſping ſomething in her arms. Lettice had the bigger child, heavy with ſleep, on her back. Miſtreſs Anne ſpake never a word.

"We muſt get indoors, uncle, as ſoon as ever we can," cried Lettice quickly.

"*Inſtanter, inſtanter,*" ſayd I, half out of my wits; "there's nobody indoors but old Meggot and his wife; and I fear they ſleep heavily."

Meanwhile we had blundered our way acroſs the ſoaked court, to the Portal, where Lettice, ſeizing the great Bell-handle, never ceaſed from pulling till the clangour reſounded through the empty Houſe. Preſently old Margery put forth her head from a Dormer window, and began in a quavering voice to cry "Murder! Fire!"

"Come down quickly," I cried, "and let us in! Here's Miſtreſs Anne!"

Margery uttered a cry of ſurpriſe, and hurried away. We ſoon heard her croſſing the Hall and undoing the Bolts. "Whatever can have brought you, good Madam, at this untimeous hour?" quod ſhe, peering into her face.

"Fire—let us have a fire quickly," ſayd Miſtreſs Anne, "and milk for the babes."

Directly Margery brought a light, I caught ſight, for the firſt time, of Miſtreſs Anne's face, and was terrified at it. Her cheeks were as crimſon, her eyes ſhining as ſtars, her wet hair hanging over her ſhoulders. From her hard, unnatural voice, and blazing eyes and cheeks, it was evident ſhe was in a high fever.

No more ſayd ſhe, but followed us ſtrait

through the great, vacant Kitchen, where we now ne'er lighted a Fire, into the Steward's Room hard by, which we preferred inhabiting and cooking in by reafon of its fnugnefs, and for Economy of Fuel. Here were dying Embers on the Hearth, which Margery fpeedily nurfed into a good Fire, Miftrefs Anne getting fo clofe to it as to endanger her garments, and fighing deeply from time to time, as fhe chafed her little infant. Margery, talking disjointedly, fet on Milk and brought Bread and Bafins, and foon they were all having bread-and-milk, and fhaking out their wet upper-garments ; and then they crept up-ftairs, where Margery made what poor provifion fhe could for their fleeping, my Lady having locked up all but the Servants' Bedding before fhe went away.

SECTION X.

Of our Journey to London.

GAT no more Sleep that night, and at Day-dawn, after counſel with Miſtreſs Anne, I ſtarted for Kelſey, to bring Sir Francis over to her.

He had juſt breakfaſted, and was playing with his Hawk when I got there. He ſayd, "What now, Moldwarp? What makes you ſo early aſtir? To pick up the early worm, eh?"

I ſayd, "Sir Francis, I have ſomewhat for your private ear. A ſore Miſchance hath befallen."

He ſayd, "Take the Hawk, Jeſſop—come in here, Nicholas;" and ſtraitway turned into his private Room; where he threw himſelf into a Chair. "Now then for it"

7

"Maſter Kyme, Sir, hath turned Miſtreſs Anne out of Doors. She came a-horſeback with her Maid and two Infants, acroſs the Moors through Wind and Rain, and reached Stallingboro' long paſt Midnight."

He ſwore an oath and ſtarted to his feet, crying, "I muſt have his Blood."

"Sir, ſir!" ſayd I, "don't talk that way . . . you have a Spouſe and two ſweet off-ſpring of your own."

"True, true," ſayd he, reſuming his ſeat. "I owe my life to my family, and a Duello does not always determine a quarrel with juſtice. But,—ſent her adrift? . . . and in ſuch Weather, too! Perhaps the illgrained fellow hath even ſtruck her!"

"She ſayd nothing of that," ſayd I.

"Well, well, then I dare ſay he has not. Moſt likely ſhe would have told if he had."

But ſhe has told nothing," ſayd I; "ſcarce opened her lips."

"That looks ſuſpicious," ſayd he, frowning and looking hard at me—"women always make enough ado in theſe caſes, and naturally make the beſt of their own cauſe, and the worſt of the other ſide. If he'd Beaten her, I vow I would draw his Blood . . . unleſs he gave me a very good reaſon indeed why I ſhould not. But we muſt be wary, Nick, we muſt be wary—there may be two ways of telling the Story; and between ourſelves, Miſtreſs Kyme's judgement is like to be warped a little by paſſion."

"But you have not heard her Story yet, Sir," cried I. "Do, for the love of ruth, ride over and ſee her for yourſelf and hear her Say. There may be things too delicate for her ſervants to be told, that ſhe will confide to a dear Brother."

"You ſay true, indeed," quod he, "and yet there is nothing on earth more diſagreeable than interference between Man and Wife—"

"But Sir! your own Siſter—'

"Or, indeed, in any Family Quarrels—"

"Turned out of Houſe and Home—"

"One is ſure to burn one's fingers- -"

"All through that drenching Rain—"

"And very likely, take the wrong ſide—"

"When I heard the Pebble come againſt my window," perſiſted I, "you might have knocked me down with a ſtraw." And then, without the manners to wait till I was bidden, I ran, or raced, through all the par.

ticulars, with fuch vehement pity and eager watchfulnefs for fome token of fympathy in him, that he could not choofe but fhow concern, and cry,

"Poor Nan! poor Nan!—truly I wifh I faw my way through this: I would confult my wife, only I know fhe would be againft my taking any rafh ftep—I muft controul myfelf—I muft feek to be mediator; Go back, Nick, and tell my Sifter I'll come over as faft as I can."

With which I was conftrained to content myfelf, though I would fain have feen him ftart when I did, fince his boiling up had fo fuddenly fubfided alreadie. However, I did him injuftice, for juft as I got back to the Hall, I heard Horfes galloping behind me, and looking round, faw him riding up, like a gallant Gentleman as he was, his white Feather ftreaming in the air, and his fine face flufhed with exercife. He flung his rein to his groom, fprang to the ground, and rufhed in with outfpread arms, crying, "My Sifter! Oh, my unhappy Sifter!"

Miftrefs Anne, rifing up from her low feat by the fire, fell into his arms, and wept tears of affection and thankfulnefs. For a

while it was only ſuch broken words as,
"Oh, my poor Nan!—that it ſhould come
to this!" "Dear, dear Frank! I knew you
would come! Oh, I have been ſo very, very
unhappy!"

"Tell me all about it," ſays he, releaſing
her from his arms, "but not in this unfit
place. Let us go into Lady Aſkew's room."
"She hath locked it up, Frank—She hath
locked up nearly all the Houſe." "Nay
then, we can pace the Hall—but you are
tired?" "In faith, Frank, I can ſcarce
ſtand—I ſhall be better preſently." And ſhe
turned deadly pale. I brought her ſome
water. "The Book-room," I ſayd, "will be
beſt."

"Juſt ſo, Nicholas," ſayd Sir Francis; and
taking his Siſter's hand, he led her in there,
and ſhut to the door. What they ſayd was
between 'emſelves alone — we could only
hear voices, raiſed to a high key ſometimes,
and then ſtifled; and a good deal of Sobbing.
It ſeemed an age before they came forth;
but they did at laſt; more by token, I think,
the Baby began to wail and ſhe heard it. I
never ſaw a deſolater Creature than ſhe looked when ſhe came forth; they were not on

the fame terms as when they went in ; and I knew what a trick he had of edging round. " Well," fays he, as if making fome great conceffion, " I'll do as I fay I will : I'll ride over and fee him : your clothes you at leaft muft have. And I hope this unhappy affair may be made up. Perchance he may this morning be in a better mind. Had he been drinking, think you ? Had you croft him in anything ? Tut, tut . . . there, don't cry. Thou knoweft, Nan, my tender love for you. Make the beft of it . . . fomething will needs come to pafs. My lady defired me to bear you her loving regards—"

" Here's my baby, Frank—you have not feen it before—"

" Ha !—" with a pre-occupied air as if it was not his firft fight of a baby ; which indeed it was not. " Well, cheer up, Sifter . . . Hope for better times . . . Receive placably the firft offer of compofition . . . Let bygones be bygones . . . he'll know better in future. Mind ye be not backward when he comes forward. Something will be arranged, I doubt not. You fhall hear from me foon. Farewell, Sifter !"

And, having embraced her anew, he fprang

into his faddle, and the white plume vanifhed
through the Gate.

The reft of the day was dull and cheer-
lefs enough ; but Miſtrefs Anne took up
her quarters in the Book-room, where I failed not to keep up a good fire, and we contrived a little fleeping place for the infants.
The eldeſt was an engaging prattler, and
amufed us whether we would or no. And·
little by little, Miſtrefs Anne relieved her
mind to me of much that was on it, and
how that a cruel Confeffor had alienated
her husband from her, even to making him
threaten her perfonal liberty, and feclufion
from her children : and fhe fayd her lot
had graduallie worfened ever fince her
father died ; and that fhe thought what had
happened now would have happened afore,
but for his having the fear of the Duchefs
of Suffolk before his eyes. She being now
at a diſtance, he had ta'en advantage of
her abfence.

When fhe ceafed, I paufed a little, and
then began gently to talk, not of her prefent
Trouble in particular, but of Troubles in
general, their purpofes, whether as judge-
ments, like the plagues of Egypt ; or chaf·

tenings, like death of David's little child;
or warnings, like the blindnefs of Elymas;
or tefts, like the fufferings of Job; or
trials, like the trials of Abraham; or puri-
fiers, like the afflictions of Mary Magdalene;
or to make the good that lay hidden in us
fhine forth with the greater luftre, as in
Queen Efther.

 When I paufed, fhe fayd, "Go on, dear
Mafter Moldwarp, I love to hear you."
Her eldeft was fleeping on a pillow, her
youngeft neftling in her arms. The day was
far fpent, the wind and rain had ceafed, we
were fitting by the fitful light of the fire.
So then, in a defultory fafhion, I moralized
on the patience of Job, and meeknefs under
contumely of Hannah, and the low eftate of
Ruth, and the trials of unloved Leah, and
the angel comforting defolate Hagar, and the
tribulations of the early Chriftians, and the
exceeding love of our Lord and Saviour in
dying for us. After this, I fayd, "Suppofe
we pray?" and knelt down that minute and
had a fpirit of utterance given me I had
never poffeffed before; and we rofe up
mightily compofed and ftrengthened. Then
the little one woke and fayd, "Sing, Mammy,

fing," and Miſtreſs Anne ſang one ſweet hymn after another. Thus, ſtrange to ſay, we were not unhappy. When we retired to reſt, after our cuſtomed devotions, ſhe gave me her hand and ſayd,—

"Oh, old Friend, how you have calmed me! Would that you were ever at hand, as aforetime." I ſayd, "Would that I were."

A few days after, a ſumptour-mule brought over ſome great ill-packed bundles of apparel moſt negligently and diſreſpectfully put together; with a billet from Sir Francis; who ſayd he had been unable to bring Maſter Kyme to any compoſition, and he believed the only way would be for his ſiſter to humble herſelf. All this time, ſhe had ſcarce taſted food ſave bread and milk; for our Board-wages neceſſitated a meagre Larder; and to ſupply ſomewhat for the unexpected demand on our reſources, I had taken up my hat, and was about to ſtep over to the Farm, when ſhe called out, "Stop the groom! I'll ride over to Kelſey. My brother is under ſome great miſapprehenſion. I was caſt forth for none other than the Goſpel's ſake. No Reproach but that of Chriſt is upon me. As for Maſter

7*

Kyme liftening to reafon, I might as well talk to the Coat-of-arms over the Gate. He hath impofed on me Silence, and threatened to gag me."

She would not be ftayed; but, equipping herfelf in cloak and muffler, fet forth accompanied by the man, leaving the children in charge of Lettice.

When the fixth morning came without her return, we became uneafy; and as the Babes wept and pined, · we planned that I fhould follow her to wit was become of her, and allege for plea, that the Infant was out of forts.

I borrowed a Horfe of my Brother, who was poffeffed of all was going on, though we kept it from the Village, and pitied us amain. When I got to Kelfey, I found Miftrefs Anne was not there: fhe had gotten a horfe and journeyed to Lincoln. What poffeft her to go to that city, I wift not, but follow her I needs muft: my Fears would let me take no reft.

When I got to Lincoln, I went to a Seed-fhop, the owner of which I knew, and afked him if he could direct me to Miftrefs Kyme. Smiling a little, he fayd, "Ye will find her in the Cathedral, ſtanding by the lectern, where ſhe hath ſtood, theſe five days, to confront, ſhe ſayth, any that ſhall allege evil againſt her   Sure. her mind muſt be ſomething diſtempered ? "

I ſayd, " Oh, believe it not.   'Tis only that ſhe hath been hardly dealt with : " and I haſtened, full of trouble, to the Cathedral, where a little knot of people were hanging about the entrance.   I paſſed through their midſt, and heard ſuch fragments as " A Beſs o' Bedlam ; "   " No, an Outcaſt Wife ; " " In ſooth a goodly Lady ; "   " A Bigot to her Opinions ; "   " A Faire Goſpeller."

When I went in, not above five or ſix people were inſide, and they were ſtanding and curiouſly ſtaring at Miſtreſs Anne where ſhe ſtoode at the lectern, calmly reading the Bible.   The ſunlight ſtreaming in upon her through a painted window at that moment, methought ſhe looked like a glorified Saint.

After waiting a good while, there was a little huſtling among the byſtanders, and one of them ſtepping up to her, uttered ſome ſorrie Jeſt, I believe, though I could not hear it, for ſhe gravely looked up at him till he turned away abaſht, and then reſumed her reading. Looking up again, however, she perceived me, and, after a moment's hesitation, reverently closed the Bible, looking round her as she did so, and saying,—

"Good Christian people, this Book containeth the words of eternal life. For holding to this Book am I now in tribulation." Then she came up to me, and eagerlie whispered, "Hath aught befallen the Children?" "The Babe," I replied, "ceases not to moan and lament." "Nay then," quod she, "I will return with thee on the instant. I have now these six days stood here, to see what would be sayd unto me; and felt not one bit afraid, because I knew my cause to be good."

Though I misdoubted her Judgement in so doing, I could not but admire her Courage and Simplicitie.

As we rode back, she told me Sir Francis had turned quite cold upon her, and shown himself of very poor spirit: adding, "They were incensed at me for awaiting and braving the evil-speakers, whose minds are set on mischief, and mightily afraid of my angering the Ecclesiastical Authorities. Howbeit, not one of them offered me let or hindrance."

After this, Sir Francis feemed minded to try what effect Neglect would have on her; for though he knew we were even pinched for food, he fent us not fo much as a difh of water fifh, though his Tenants were bound to fupply his table with 'em all the year round; and though, when fhe depended not on Prefents for Plenty, fcarce a week paffed without gifts of Game, Fruit, and fuchlike, going to Mafter Kyme's houfe.

Miftrefs Anne felt the unkindnefs very little, for in truth fhe feemed not to know what fhe ate or drank, and fhe preferred Bread-and-milk, becaufe 'twas foon lapt up and caufed no Flufhings nor Heavinefs.

Her time was now mainly fpent in Letter-writing, to I think almoft every member of her family, and alfo to friends at a diftance; and the counfel they fent her was fo diverfe, that if fhe had been fo minded fhe could not have followed it at all. Sir Francis at length came over again to his fifter; and was moft contrary and querimonious, alleging that as fhe had brewed, fo fhe muft bake; that Mafter Kyme would on no hand now receive her again into his Houfe. She fayd, deeply fighing, "Since that is fo, I muft fue for a divorce." "I thought you would fay it," quod Sir Francis. "You were beft to apply to Coufin Britain, for you have not much to go towards law charges." She fayd, "Will you write to him about it?" He fayd, "I fhall neither make nor meddle in the matter." "Oh, well, then I muft do it myfelf," fhe fayd calmly; and fhe wrote to Mafter Britain, a very compofed and well-ordered letter. He had for fome time been a husband and a father, and was rifing into fair practice.

By the earlieft opportunity came a letter from Mafter Britain, fhowing what real fympathy could be, and what real friendfhip could offer. He expreffed great tribulation at her fad cafe, much indignation againft Mafter Kyme, to whom he offered to write, and he begged in his Wife's name and his own, that fhould fhe refort to London, fhe would, in any cafe, lodge in his houfe.

Miftrefs Anne would not be beholden to him for this, nor cumber him and his good wife with herfelf and fmall children: but fhe felt the goodnefs none the lefs, and fayd it joyed her heart. Alfo he had fent her her quarterly payment, which he took fhame to

himſelf for not having aſcertained beforetime
that ſhe had punctually received. Thus,
with money in her purſe, ſhe was able to
provide for the journey ; and ſhe reſolved to
ſet forth without delay.

Now when I beheld the dear young Lady
thus about to be thrown on the world,
without any of the male kind to care whether ſhe ſhould ſink or ſwim, I determined to
be her attendant. After a little debate, ſhe
conſented to this, thanking me much beyond
my deſerts or wiſhes ; and my Brother, ſtill
helpful in every way he could, provided us
with Horſes and a Guide : Miſtreſs Anne
and her Maid each carrying a child, and
riding Pillion.

SECTION XI.

Of what befel us in London.

T an Inn on the Road, where we baited, a flovenly Fellow lounging about the place feemed watching us attentively, and Miftrefs Anne, happening to notice him, fay'd to me, " That man comes fometimes to Mafter Kyme." He, feeing himfelf obferved, lounged away; but I faw him again, juft before we entered London, and thought he dogged us.

Arrived in the City, we found a plain but decent Lodging with an old fervant, over againft the Temple, where was a double-bedded Chamber for Miftrefs Anne, the Infants, and my Niece; a Parlour, and an Attic for myfelf. She foon took order for

the method of her ſmall Houſehold on a
ſcale proportioned to her means ; and having written letters to Maſter Britain and
two Ladies of her acquaintance, ſent me
forth to deliver them.   It ſeemed ſtrange to
me to be blundering my way about the
buſie City, the noiſes of which bewildered
me ; howbeit I did mine errands at laſt,
though more tardily than if I had been uſed
to London. Maſter Britain was conferring
with a Client, but when he ſaw me, his
countenance changed ; and as ſoon as the
Client was gone, he made me ſit down and
go over the whole matter in a plaine,
methodicall way.

"I always thought Kyme a Churl," quod
he, " but gueſſed not he would exhibit this
extremity of Malice. What is the ground
of it, think ye ? "

I ſayd it undoubtedlie had been arouſed by
diverſitie of religious Belief.

"There is no more likelie Cauſe. I con
feſs I ſee not my way through this matter
Separation is a grievouſe remedy, and yet,
e'en if we could bring them together
again, we could not make them more of a
mind."

He fayd he would ftep round in the after-noon and fee his Coufin, and invite her to vifit his Wife at Chelfea. When I went back, I found Miftrefs Anne tying on her hood : fhe fayd the miftrefs of the houfe, Miftrefs Berry, was going to hear a Lecture, and had offered to take her with her. So I followed, to take care of both.

The Lecture was given by one Porter, a godly preacher, in the Crypt of St. Paul's. It gave us matter for much difcourfe and fearching of Scripture on our return ; and while thus engaged, there came in Mafter Britain. He was more affected at the meet-ing, I thought, than fhe ; for her mind was now ftrung up and fixed on Matters far above the little reverfes of daily life. When fhe told him where fhe had been, he fayd he had heard Mafter Porter once or twice him-felf, and deemed highly of him, but that attendance on his Lectures was not without danger, for that a retrograde movement had taken place in the King's Government under the influence of Gardiner, Wriothefley, and the Duke of Norfolk. She fayd, " Are we to fall back becaufe of them ? " He fayd, " No, but he had no mind to put his head in

the lion's mouth, and hoped ſhe would not."
She replied not whether or no.

Then he bade her to Chelſea ; but when
ſhe found Miſtreſs Britain was keeping her
bed, ſhe ſayd ſhe would defer it to a more
convenient time. Then they got to her
matter with Maſter Kyme, and ſhe was very
quiet about it, and did not ſay aught that
was querimonious. She ſayd they could not
fort 'emſelves together : ſhe had known from
the firſt they had their minds ſet oppoſite
ways, and 'twas conſcience with her not to
change hers. He ſayd, " And perchance with
Maſter Kyme too." She ſayd, when it came
to being a Man's conſcience to lock up his
Wife, threaten to gag her and ſeparate her
from her Children, and tell her Servants they
were not to liſten to her nor heed what ſhe
ſayd, it was not eaſy to live with him. But
when he put her outſide the Door amid rain
and darkneſs, and refuſed to let her in again,
ſhe could not chooſe but live without him.

Maſter Britain brooded over this in painful
ſilence.

" So the Law had beſt complete what he
hath begun," ſhe ſayd quietly. " Then I ſhall
know where I am."

"Not in a hurry, not in a hurry," fayd he. "Nothing will be gained by precipitation."

"What am I to live on?"

"Of courfe we fhall take order about that."

"Very well, then," fayd fhe, fighing, "I fhall leave it to your direction."

"And where fhall you abide?"

"Where, better than here?"

"This is but a poor place."

"The fitter for poor fortunes—I care not a Pin," added fhe quickly, "for living on Bread-and-milk. *Do* I, Moldwarp?"

"Mafter Nicholas," fayd he, cordially, "I am right glad you have linked yourfelf to my Coufin's fortunes."

When he was gone, we had our frugal fupper: at Evenfong, the good woman of the houfe, whofe intereft Miftrefs Anne had quickly fecured, came in to join in the family exercifes, which Miftrefs Anne conducted, reading the portion of Scripture, praying, and leading the Pfalmody. After this, we all went peaceably to reft.

There was always fome lecture or fermon, or prayer-meeting to attend. In the morning a man in violet-coloured livery brought a note from Lady Denny, faying fhe was going down the river to the Court at Greenwich, and inviting Miftrefs Anne to bear her company: the Man would attend her to the Barge. I attended her to it too, and faw her fafe into my Lady's hands: fhe was too fair to fee and unufed to City ways to be let go hither and thither.

When fhe returned, Lady Denny's groom of the chamber, Chriftopher, faw her to the door, and fhe was forry fhe could only give him a groat. But the day arrived when the groat came from him to her.

She looked bright, and fayd, "Oh, they were all fo good, I have been almoft happy! I have been with Lady Hertford, and fhe is a very Saint. Her whole ftudy is the Bible."

After this, fhe was fent for by thefe and other Court ladies from time to time, and enjoyed delices of Chriftian friendfhip and converfation. The reft of her time was fpent quite in a retired manner with her children, only going forth to hear Lectures and Sermons. All this while, Sir Francis wrote only once to her, without figning his name at full length; but Miſtreſs Diſney wrote twice and kindly.   Meſeemed, her own Sex ſympathized with her a good deal the moſt.   Mayhap the married men feared her enſample, as the privy council of King Ahaſuerus feared that of Queen Vaſhti.   But they need not to have been afeard of Miſtreſs Anne.

The more I held converſe with her, the more I perceived how her powers of reflec‑ tion and reaſoning had ripened ſince her Marriage; which was not ſo much by the ſtudy of many books as of one Book, and making divine paſture thereon.

One day, my Niece ſayd unto me, " Me‑ thought People in great Cities were leſs curious than in ſmall Villages, and had leſs time for their Neighbours' Affairs."

" 'Tis ſo," I replied.

" There's One i' the next Houſe," returned Lettice, " whoſe ſole Buſineſſe ſeems to be to watch us from Morn till Night."

" Aye ? " quoth I.   " The man that dogged us on the Road ? "

" No, not he, though he may be ſet on by him.   If, when thou returneſt home, thou lookeſt up at the firſt-floor Lattice,

there thou ſhalt ſee him, lurking juſt within
the ſhadow, like a Spider watching for a
Fly."

I did ſo, and liked not the look of the
Fellow, who caught my eye and drew back.
Thereafter I made it my buſineſs to ſtare
hard at him, every time I came back, till
I'm ſure he hated the very ſight of me. At
my inſtance, Miſtreſs Berry privily aſked the
woman next door whether ſhe had let her
lodging and who was her Lodger. She ſayd,
one Maſter Wadloe, a Curſitor of Chancery,
and a man of great piety. However, his
piety proved to be of the ſort Saul of Tarſus
had, when he haled poor Chriſtians to priſon.
It came out afterward, that, having gathered
ſomewhat of her ſtory, after a twiſted faſhion,
and not thinking well of her Life, he had
been ſo officious as to get himſelf lodged next
Door, for the main or ſole intent to ſpy out
her ways, and ſift them fine.

But mark the Iſſue of this: and take
Comfort therein. From her malicious Eſ-
pion, he became a compleat Convert to her
virtue and ſanctity. For, ſayd he afterward,
" She is the moſt devout and godly creature
that ever I knew. At midnight ſhe begin-

neth to pray, and ceaſeth not for a long while after, when I and others apply our-ſelves to ſleape or do worſe."

Now befel the ſad and ſorrowful caption of Maſter Porter the Bible reader, who was committed to Newgate by order of Bonner, to the grievouſe loſs and lamentation of his well-wiſhers and diſciples. Maſter Britain's ſecond viſit to us was made as touching this, and to warn off Miſtreſs Anne from ſhowing herſelf openly his follower. Whereon ſhe quoted, "I was ſick and in priſon and you viſited me;" and aſked him how he inter-preted that. He ſayd, that was ſpoken to Men. She ſayd, "I've yet to learn there's one Goſpel for Men and another for Women." In truth, ſhe with Miſtreſs Berry, and me for their Uſher. had already been to Newgate, and there cheered the priſoner's heart with Scriptural comfort. On his part, he was no whit caſt down or amazed, but lifted up his voice and preached the Saviour till e'en the Gaolers melted.

The end of this poor young Man, though painful, was ſhort. On the plea of cauſing tumultuous Aſſemblages, e'en in Priſon, he was caft into a Lower Dungeon, and there chained by the Neck to the Wall; through which hard treatment, he, though young and vigorous, was, on the eighth day, found dead in his Bonds.

Then came to pafs that which Mafter Britain in his world-fapience had predicted; to wit that Miftrefs Anne, having been noted beyond others, maybe on account of her excellent Beauty, as having reforted to Newgate and upheld him in the Faith, was fummoned before the Queft affembled at Sadlers' Hall, for having broken the law of the Six Articles. I, having fcarce time to ftart off after her, haftily bade Miftrefs Berry advife Mafter Britain of the event.

I fcarce need to tell anie well-inftructed perfon that the Six prefcribed Articles of Faith, lately impofed on all by Act of Parliament through ye Influence of that Bigot the Duke of Norfolk, were thefe :—1. The Corporal prefence of Chrift in the elements. 2. Reception of the Communion in one kind. 3. Vows of Chaftity. 4. Private Maffes. 5. Celibacy of the Clergy. 6. Auricular Confeffion.

Againft moft of thefe Cranmer had argued

8

for several days. But the Popish party were as five to four; so they carried it.

In the greatest of Trouble I now took my way to Sadlers' Hall, where, on entering, I found Christopher Dare, being one of the Quest, examining her on the Real Presence, and putting it to her, did she believe the Sacrament hanging over the Altar was Christ's very body or not.

Then she: "I will in like manner ask you a Question, and do you answer me: Why was St. Stephen stoned to death?"

He frowned and pished, and could not think of an apt reply, and sayd he could not tell.

"No more tell I you what you have asked me," sayd she.

"It hath been alleged against you," quod he, "that you have been heard to say, 'God dwelleth not in temples made with hands.'"

"Well," then sayd she, "how read you the seventh and seventeenth chapters of the Acts of the Apostles? What say St. Stephen and St. Paul therein?"

"Nay," sayth he, "I have not their words at my fingers' end."

" Theſe be they," ſayd ſhe—" Sayth Stephen
(Acts ſeven, forty-eight) 'Howbeit the Moſt
High dwelleth not in temples made with
hands : as ſayth the Prophet, Heaven is my
throne and earth is my footſtool : what houſe
will ye build Me? ſayth the Lord : or what is
the place of my reſt? Hath not my hand
made all theſe things ?'—Holy Stephen quoted the prophet Iſay : chapter ſixty-ſix. Hear
alſo what St. Paul ſayth : Acts ſeventeen—
'God, that made the world and all things
therein, ſeeing that he is Lord of Heaven
and earth, dwelleth not in temples made
with hands ; neither is worſhipped with
men's hands, as though he needeth anie
thing, ſeeing he giveth to all, life and breath
and all things.' "

" Well," ſayth he, looking ſomething mazed,
" how take ye theſe ſentences ?"

On which ſhe, with the only little daſh of
impatience from firſt to laſt, ſayd—" I will not
throw pearls before ſwine ; acorns are good
enow for them."

After a pauſe, he aſked her,

" How came you to ſay, ' I had rather
read five lines in the Bible than hear five
maſſes ?' "

"Well, I *would* rather," fhe fayd quiet-lie.

"How fo ?"

"Not for the difpraife of the Epiftle or Gofpel, but becaufe the one would greatly edify me, the other not at all."

"How? Not at all?"

"Doth not St. Paul witnefs in the four-teenth chapter of his firft epiftle to the Corinthians, faying, 'If the trumpet giveth an uncertain found, who will prepare himfelf for the battle?'"

"Oh, then you maintain that if an ill Prieft miniftereth, 'tis the fubftance of the devil, and not of God."

Then fhe: "I never fayd fo; nor did I mean it. The ill-conditions of the Prieft that miniftered could nohow hurt my faith. In fpirit I fhould ftill receive the body and blood of Chrift."

"What haft thou to fay, as touching Con-feffion ?"

"The fame that St. James fayd, that every man ought to acknowledge his faults to others, and pray, the one for the other."

"What is your judgement of the King's book ?"

"Nay, I can form no judgement, tor I have never read it!"

Dare feemed to have come to his wit's end, for he now fent for a Prieſt noted for a Zealot.

He, in place of dodging her after the previous unſkilled faſhion, held to one main point, and preſſed her hard down upon it. What deemed ſhe of the Sacrament of the Altar?

She, perceiving him for what he was, one that would fain entangle her in her talk, fayd only, "I pray you have me excuſed."

He prefented the queſtion to her again in various forms; but ſhe returned no other anfwer. At this junċture, I heard a hard breathing clofe behind me, and looking round, beheld Maſter Britain, gazing and liſtening with the utmoſt anxiety.

Then fayd the Prieſt, "Believeſt thou not, that private Maſſes help departed Souls? Anfwer thou me."

To whom ſhe anfwered, "It were indeed idolatry, to believe more in them than in the death which Chriſt died for us miferable finners."

I drew a deep ſigh, and 'twas echoed beſide me. Then ſayd Chriſtopher Dare, with a geſture of impatience, " There is no arguing with ſuch a woman—ſhe muſt be brought before the Lord Mayor."

It might have been thought a matter of dailie courſe to her to be brought before him, ſo compoſedly did ſhe go forth to appear before him and the Common Council then ſitting in Guildhall.

My Lord Mayor, Sir Martin Bowes by name, a goldſmith of good Yorkſhire family, might be reaſonably ſuppoſed no rare theologian. He put to her the futile and irreverend queſtion that had alreadie been mooted along with many other Quodlibets, as touching a Mouſe that ſhould eat the Hoſt : adding, " What ſayeſt thou, fooliſh Woman ? "

Thereat Miſtreſs Anne did not refrain from ſmiling ; and ſundrie of the Council laughed outright, which made the Lord Mayor ſore diſpleaſed.

" Tell me, woman," quod the Chancellor of London, " haſt thou not by word of mouth publicly addreſſed congregations contrary to Scripture ? "

" No, on my faith," ſayth ſhe.

It came into my mind that he muſt have heard ſome Bruit of her ſtanding by the Lectern in Lincoln Cathedral, before the face of all the people. Sad to relate, though her anſwers gave or ſhould have given full ſatiſſaction, they had no mind to be ſatiſſyde; whereby this faire and innocent Lady, by nature ſhamefaſt, by education cultivated, of habits retired and unacquainted with the world, was ſent to the Comptor priſon in Bread Strete, the Lord Mayor refuſing to take bail.

A mob of men and boys, moſtly City Prentices, hung about the grated window whence the Priſoners could look forth. Lettice and I did the ſame, albeit with ſmall expectance that Miſtreſs Anne would ſhow her dear face at it. However, when we heard the priſoners begging a few pence of the by-ſtanders to buy bread, and apprehended that our own dear Lady might e'en want food with the reſt, we ſearched our pouches, but alas, found not ſo much as a Genoa halfpenny therein. On this, Lettice, with a hardihood for which I ſincerely commend her, went up to the keen-looking lads and accoſted them with, "Of your pity, fair young Sirs, a trifle for my good Miftrefs; and may ye never, never know what it is to want a Cruft of Bread!"

On this, with the impulfivenefs of youth, they abfolutely fhowered fmall coin on her, till, I believe, they had none left; fhe thanking and blefling them with more fluency than I could have commanded, had my Life depended on it. Then fhe would have handed the money through the grate, but the villainous expreffion of fome of the faces looking forth, made her diftruftful. At length a good, pious man, whom we knew by fight, received it of her, and promifed it fhould go to her Lady.

Oh, where was Sir Francis, the loved companion of her youth (that bade her face the Bull and ran away himfelf)? where was the Husband of her Efpoufals, who had promifed to cherifh and fuccour her till Death fhould them part?

As well afk for laft Summer's Gnats. The fair Creature was utterly left to her own Difcretion and Faithfulnefs; which, fo fupporting her as they did, made it clear to all but the wilfully blind, that grace was given her from On High. She looked unto the Hill from whence came her help; and the Lord, in place of removing her Trial, ſupported her under it.

8*

SECTION XII.

Of our Change of Place.

 HOW were we ftruck through as with a dart, when the Prifon Door clofed on our loved Miftrefs Anne! We went back to our Lodging the wretchedeft fouls on earth, there to be affailed by a flood of importunate Queftions from the Woemen, and floods of Tears and bitter Lamentations, in the which I fhame not to fay I joined. By and by, I bade them call to mind how that when Peter was caft into Prifon, prayer was made without ceafing of the Church unto God for him; and that it was while they were engaged, late at night in that very act, that he was delivered unto them, even by the hand of an Angel, fo that

the Servant-maid Rhoda, hearing his voice at the Gate, opened it not for gladnefs, but ran in to tell the reft. And I improved Miftrefs Anne's command of the Scriptures, chapter and verfe and word for word, and fhowed how they were the Sword of the Spirit that man could neither gainfay nor refift, though he could gag the mouth that fpoke them. Thereafter we gave ourfelves the greater part of the night to Prayer, and many enfuing nights and days our Minds were continually in a fupplicating pofture before the Lord, pleading with Him His own Promifes, and acknowledging we were not worthy to Afk what yet we befought him to per-form.

At the end of twelve days, I learned from Mafter Britain, to whom I made dailie refort, that he had obtained leave to fee her and concert with her meafures for her Releafe on bail. I waited for him outfide, and when he came forthe, his face looked full of care. He told me Bifhop Bonner had fent a Prieft unto her, to prove her with hard queftions, and that her matter was now handed over to the Eccleftaftical Court. She was to go before the Bifhop next day.

When I repeated this to the Woemen they begun to lament and ſay, "Alas, for us, our prayers are not heard." I ſayd, "Ye ſilly ſouls, there is more need for prayer than ever: be at it without ceaſing; perchance it may draw a Bleſſing and not a Curſe."

So they took pattern by the importunate Widow, and ſpared not their pleadings, Day nor Night. Meantime the Biſhop of London having told Maſter Britain that anie of the Priſoner's friends might be preſent at her examination the day following, he ſent off expreſſes to her Brothers, and to her Huſband, if haply his Heart might be ſoftened. But they came not, and indeede Time woulde have failed, if Inclinacion had not. To be briefe, no one ſhowed friendlie to her, but Maſter Britain and my unworthy ſelf; and I had no Bail to offer, and only went to ſee and hear all I coulde, how the matter would turn, and remained in the Lobby, while Maſter Britain went in. Meanwhile a friend of his, one Maſter Spelman of Gray's Inn, arrived at his inſtance, to be her Surety, ſhould no kinſman appear.

They waited as long as they could for her Brothers, and the Biſhop bade Maſter Britain exhort her meantime, to reveal freely the ſecrets of her heart when ſhe came to be examined, for that, whatever ſhe ſhould ſay, in his Houſe, no man ſhould hurt her for it. This, Biſhop Bonner repeated to her himſelf, when he went in to ſee her privately ; ſhowing none of that Severity and Ruthleſſneſs he afterward made manifeſt.

All being ready (ſave the kindred that ne'er came) Miſtreſs Anne was brought before the Court with proper order ; and the Biſhop began examining her on the Sacrament. Attaining to no ſatiſſactory Iſſue thereby, the Biſhop went out, anon returning with a written Paper, to which he deſired her to ſign her Name. She, looking at what was writ, before ſigning, ſayd,

" I believe ſo much thereof as the book of Scripture doth agree to."

On this, he ſhortly replyed, " It is not for you to teach me what to write."

Then ſhe, taking the pen which was given her, wrote, " I Anne Aſkew do believe all manner of thynges contayned in the faith of the Catholic Church."

When the Biſhop ſaw what was writ, he waxed red with choler, and riſing up from

his feat, went forthe into his withdrawing-
room. Thither followed him Mafter Britain
and Doctor Wefton, and found him in a rage
with the perverfeft creature he had known in
his life. Sayd Mafter Britain—

"O my Lord! fet not her weak woman's
witt againft your Lordfhip's great wifdom!"
—and Doctor Wefton fayd other mollyfying
things ; fo that, in fine, ye Bifhop was
brought to releafe his victim that time on
Bail. Howbeit, fhe was ftill detained two
more days in Cuftody, (which gave her
younger Brothers time to have come) till fhe
fhould agayn appear before the civil! authorities in Guildhall. Then fhe finally obtayned
her Difcharge in the Confiftory Court of St.
Paul's ; her coufin Britain and Mafter Spelman being Sureties for her future appearance
if it were required.

And thus we got her back. Our eyes
were filled with Tears of joy rather than our
mouths with laughter, at her fo great deliverance ; and there was not one of us fayd,
"Why obtayned ye not fooner Releafe?"
She was free and yet fhe had yielded not a
jot ; for the claufe fhe appended to her Name
bare witnefs that fhe had never recanted.

Bonner, meanwhile, might boaſt, an' he would, of having got her ſignature—he knew what that addition ſignified, and forgat it not nor forgave.

When ſhe came forth, I lookt to ſee her faire Face marred with grief and Terror : having nightly pictured her to myſelf lying alone and in Darkneſſe, in ſome Mean Cell, her Spiritts amazed and dejected. On the contrary, though her Raiment (which was of Black) was ſoiled with duſt, her Face, engaging as a Child's, looked all Peace and Sweetneſs ; and almoſt her firſt word to me, after learning how fared the Infants, was—

" O, dear friend ! I have found that Thing which I deſired, but wiſt not would ever be vouchſafed me—ſomething to do and to ſuffer for God. Since He hath counted me worthy to bear teſtimony for Him, there is nothing I ſhall love ſo much to do unto my Life's end, He being my Helper."

I ſayd, " Beſeech ye, Miſtreſs, be careful, for the young Babes' ſakes."

She ſayd, " I ſeemed, in priſon, to feel their little Fingers twining round mine. Careleſs I may not be ; cowardly will I

never be. I brought not my Trial on myfelf, anie more than anie that reforted to
Porter in Newgate ; and I anfwered the
Queft to the beft of my judgement. I did
not force the Truth on them, they forced it
from me. Should they tear me with red-
hot pincers, they will get nothing elfe."
And fhe added that the lads of Sparta could
bear to be whipped before the Altars, without
fo much as quecking.

When I fayd Sir Francis fhould have come,
her face changed, and fhe fayd, "Ah, he might
ha' come, an' he would."

I fayd, "Maybe my Lady would not let
him."

"Coufin Britain," quod fhe, "did not fail
me like my Brothers."

'Twas pretty to fee her fly to her children
and fondle them, and they neftling in her
arms, to fmother her with kiffes ; but foon
fhe fayd fhe muft change her prifon-foiled
garments. Oh! what Thankfgivings rofe
from our full hearts that Night. When the
Infants were a-Bed, fhe took her Lute, and
fang a fweet Hymn fhe had compofed in her
imprifonment.

Thereafter, we had three months of peace-

fulle reſt : and, for that we were driven to
hard ſhift, ſometimes, for our daily Meat, ſo
ſcant were her Means, I betook me to em-
blazon ſundrie Samples of Ornamental Pen-
manſhip, which raiſed a few Shillings.
We never abounded and we never lacked.
Miſtreſs Anne was ſent for once and agayn
by Lady Hertford and Lady Denny, the
Counteſs of Suſſex, and the Ducheſs of Suffolk, and I played the Uſher to her when ſhe
went to Greenwich, albeit my well-bruſhed
Suit was too threadbare to find favour in the
ſcornful eyes of the Waiters in the ante-
chamber. On one occaſion, that gracious
child, the Lady Jane Grey, then nine years
old, did run after her as ſhe came forth, and
ſay in a low voice, "Oh, Miſtreſs Aſkew,
the Queen wiſhes to ſee the book you ſpoke
of."

For her grace Queen Katherine Parr was
herſelf an illuſtrious Reformer, and had ap-
pointed Miles Coverdale her Almoner, and
commiſſioned Nicholas Udall, Maſter of Eton
ſchool, to edit the Tranſlations of Eraſmus
his Paraphraſes of the four Goſpels ; e'en
inciting her royal ſtep-daughter, Princeſs
Mary, to accept its dedication : the Queen

being then at Hanworth. And the Lady
Herbert and Lady Tyrrell, and young Lady
Jane Grey, all of her privy-chamber, were all
of 'em Reformers, and fearched the Scriptures diligently in the fpirit of the Bereans.
Wherefore it is eafie to conclude with what
zeft they hearkened unto her who now was
called The Faire Gofpeller, and who had en-
dured bond and imprifonment for the Truth
as it is in Jefus.

This good countenance toward her could
not be hid in a corner. And albeit, when
fhe went to the Palace, fhe was had into the
privy-chamber where none overheard her
talk with her Majefty and the Honorable
women : it became furmized and whifpered
among the houfehold, that Miftrefs Anne
ftood high in royal regard. All this while
her family held clofe, in their Country-feats,
and gave no fignal of Love or Remem-
brance.

In the month of June, woe worth the hour !
fhe was fummoned again before the Council in
Guildhall, along with Miftrefs Joan Santery,
and Robert Luken, fervant of Sir Humphrey
Brown. But nought being proven againft
them, they were all difcharged ; only one

witneſs appearing againſt Luken, and he
ſeeming influenced by malice. Great was
our thankfulneſs to have Miſtreſs Anne once
more reſcued from the Lions' Den ; this time
alſo, ſhe had made no temporizing con-
ceſſion, neither damaged herſelf by any
ſelf-accuſation. She offended not with the
tongue.

Maſter Britain payd her Quarterage punc-
tuallie, and, knowing how hard a matter we
had to live, would have preſſed on her money
of his own ; but ſhe would none of it, ſaying, if her Husband and Brothers would do
as they ought, ſhe need be beholden to nobody, and if they would not, ſhe would make
ſhift with that ſhe had. Indeed, never Lady
made ſo little ſuffice as ſhe did : her linen
and cambric, of the fineſt, carefully waſhed
and mended by Lettice, wanted hitherto no
additions : ſhe had one or two black gowns
for morning wear, and a deep Black Velvet
for Court, on which her long, taper, jewel-
led fingers looked like wax. Her ſmall
white ruff and wriſt cuffs were broidered
with red—emblem of that red and fiery
burning in which her fair body was afterwards conſumed. Thoſe Ladies her friends

would have ſupplyed her handſomely with aught ſhe needed, but ſhe would never take of them.

One day when I attended her to Greenwich, and was awaiting her in the anteroom, which of all places I count the moſt tedious, a flippant hanger-on, with ſubtle malice in his long, narrow, ill-favoured face, croſſed the room to me on the pointed tips of his toes, and beſpoke me with—

"By your favour, Sir; what think you of theſe vext queſtions?"

"I know not of what you ſpeak," quod I.

"Of theſe Six Articles, and ſuch like."

"Oh," ſayd I.   "Thoſe are queſtions that ſeem to invite no anſwer. They may vex ſundrie, but I know not how they can be vext."

"You are guarded," ſayd he.

"Are not you ſo?" ſayd I.   "Every man had better be: eſpeciallie a King's Penſioner. Look here," pulling a copy of my Treatyſe from my pouch, "here's a little work writ by my unworthie pen, for which I receive the King's bounty to this day. The Print, you ſee, is Fine: the Topic not uninter·eſting. A few copies are ſtill on hand at the

Bible and Crown, if you ſhould pleaſe to take one."

"Thanks," ſayd he; going off quicker than he came. Thereafter, when anie of 'em ſeemed about to accoſt me with trouble-ſome intent, I took the whip-hand of 'em by inviting them to ſubſcribe to a new edition of my Book dedicated to the King. They ſoon ſhunned me like contagion.

About this time, I had a noteworthy Dream. I ſay not there was aught ſuper-natural in it, but at any rate it notably fore-ſhadowed events. Methought Miſtreſs Anne was walking on a fair Terrace by a River ſide, with one of thoſe devout Ladyes, and that anon they ſate down on a ſtone Bench and continued converſing, though I heard not one word that they ſayd. Meanwhile the darkneſs of Evening gradually ſtole on, and I continued to watch with pleaſure the motion of their lips, their earneſt, pretty geſtures, and the concern diſplayed in their countenances. Looking up, I beheld in the deep purple Firmament a little twinkling Star, juſt beginning to be born, as 'twere, in the blue expanſe. Beholding it fixedly, I ſaw it wax bigger and brighter, deſcending gradually towards Miſtreſs Anne, till at length it diſcloſed itſelf as a glorious Crown, and encircled her Head . . whereon I woke.

Yet month followed month, and ſtill we dwelt in peace.

One day, I was croſſing Lincoln's Inn Fields, when I almoſt ran againſt Sir Francis. He turned quite white when he ſaw who I was ; though, at the moment, he had clapped his hand on his Sword. I was equally ſtartled, but made my Obeiſance, and ſayd, " Sir Francis, Miſtreſs Anne will rejoice to ſee you."

" Forbear to mention names," interrupted he, quickly. " Call me plain Sir, and ſpeak of her as your Miſtreſs. What makes ſhe now. How fares ſhe ? "

" As poorly as ſhe well can, having ſcarce cheeſe to her bread."

" Tut, tut! to whom is it owing ? She hath brought it on herſelf. What a fine meſs ſhe got into, being ſhut up in the Comptor ! 'Tis no very pleaſant thing for a gentleman of my Poſition to hear talked of, I can tell thee. She ſhould think of her Kindred a little."

"And her Kindred of her, Sir," ſayd I. He looked fiercely at me, but I would not be put down.

"Oh!" ſayd I, "how you once loved her!——"

He was turning on his Heel; but ſtopped.

"You drive me out of my mind," ſayd he, impatiently. "Attend to what I am about to ſay, Nicholas. A freſh Hereſy Bill hath paſſed, the meſhes of which are not ſo wide but my Siſter may be caught in it. Let her take warning betimes, and be ruled for her ſafety. Inſtead of hanging about the Court (a moſt unſeemlie practice for a married woman ſeparated from her husband) let her reſume the old ſhamefaſtneſs and quietneſs, which, as you ſay, once made her ſo dear to me. I know of a ſafe Retreat, where ſhe may harbour, an' if ſhe will, till this preſent danger be overpaſt. Do you think ſhe will have ſenſe enow to abide in it——?"

"With me, and her Children, and her Maid, Sir?"

"Aye, all of you. Is ſhe ſcant of money?"

"She hath ſcarce anie."

"Why has not Britain advanced her forme?"

"She would not have it."

"Tilly-vally. Well, I will allow you, Nicholas, so much by the week. You used to bear the Purse when we travelled, and were a pretty fair Accountant. I will allow you so much for the whole family by the Week, payable to yourself through Mafter Britain, as long as she will accept the covert, and abide in it. Do you clofe with the offer?"

"As far as I can, Sir, for another: and thankfully."

"Well, try to get her to do the fame: and let me know."

"Will you not fee her, Sir?"

"No, by no means. It would affect me too much. Come hither to-morrow, at this hour—Nay, go to Mafter Britain's chamber, that will be beft. Tell him; and he will tell you."

Saying which he waved his hand, and fwung out of fight with the white Feather ftreaming from his fmart Beaver.

When I told Miftrefs Anne I had feen him, her colour changed, and tears came into her eyes. She fayd—"Why came not

dear Frank near me? Where is he? I'll
go to him."

" He told not where he was," ſayd I, "and
apparently wiſhed us not to know. Elſe, why
interpoſe a third party?"

" What doſt thou adviſe me to do, Moldwarp?"

" In faith, Madam, what good do you
here? Your matter with Maſter Kyme is
no more advanced. Your means are almoſt
extinct: you will not borrow of friends.
You ſayd nobody ſhould help you but your
Husband or your Brother. Be helped, then,
by your Brother."

" Sayd he what his help would be?"

" No; but he ſayd it ſhould ſuffice for
all."

After meditating a little, ſhe ſayd, " Well
then, ſo let it be. Having but food and
raiment, let us therewith be content. I care
not how removed the Retreat is, ſo I have
my Children."

So I carried her acquieſcence to Maſter
Britain, who ſeemed mighty relieved by it;
and he gave me the firſt inſtallment of our
allowance, which was ſtill ſmaller than I
had looked for; and ordayned that we ſhould

make up our Fardels and be ready to ſtart in a vehicle that ſhould be provided before day-dawn, at a certain place.

SECTION XIII.

Of what befel us there.

UR Retreat, out of fight of Men or found of hoof or wheel, was rufticall enow to be a pleafing exchange to us countrie-bred Folk from the noife of Temple Bar, the din of Church-bells, hoarfe cries of Wagoners, fhrill calls of Fifhwomen and Milkmaids, whooping and whiftling of city-prentices, with now and then the fhouts of " Clubs ! clubs !" When Spring fhould come it would be good for the little ones to fmell the breath of cows, and ftray about the meadow gathering daifies and buttercups ; and meanwhile we had an inexpreffible fenfe of peace and fafetie.

Mafter Britain had advanced me a month's

Allowance ; and when I went to him for the ſecond, he told me things were going ill with the Reformers, and leſt I ſhould be trackèd, he would pay me a Quarter's allowance, and we had better keep as ſnug as · we could through the Winter ; which we did. When I next went to him, he told me anie breach of the Six Articles was being eagerly laid hold of by ye Council, in ſpecial when anie perſons of note laid themſelves open to ſuſpicion. " Therefore," ſayth he, " keep my Couſin as quiet as ye can, and let us hope ſhe may be overlookt."

As the Spring advanced, he told me Doctor Latimer and Doctor Crome had been had up for examination, and that two of his Majeſty's perſonal attendants, ſat George Blaage (whom the King called Piggy) and John Laſcelles, were impriſoned.

" 'Tis thought matters will go hard with 'em," quod he ; " and e'en the Queen's ladies are imperillèd, nay, e'en the Queen herſelf ; ſo be more careful of my Couſin than ever."

I did not ſee how I could, but promiſed I would take all the care in my power. Afterwards I went to good Miſtreſs Berry, with whom we had lodged at Temple Bar. She ſayd ſhe was both glad and ſorrie to ſee me : glad to ſee the face of a friend ; forry that my coming to her might lead to my being tracked ; " for," ſayth ſhe, " this houſe is ſtill being watched from next door ; and inquiry hath lately been made after you."

I told Miſtreſs Anne this with trouble, but ſhe calmly ſayd, " Be not diſmayed : not a hair of our heads ſhall fall without per- miſſion of our Heavenly Father." We gave ourſelves much unto prayer ; but I obſerved, that, while I prayed for her Deliverance from all Dangers ghoſtly and bodilie, ſhe only prayed for faith and ſubmiſſion, and direction, and ſtrength to fulfil the Lord's will, and pro- tection for her Children.

One night, juſt at Bed-time, there was a rapping at the Door ; and on my opening it, a lad thruſt a Billet into my hand, and fled. It bore no ſuperſcription, but contained theſe words in Sir Francis' hand, diſ- guiſed—

" Your Retreat is, I fear, diſcovered. Flee to the place you wot of, without the Children. They ſhall be cared for."

I gave it to Miſtreſs Anne, for whom

'twas meant.   She changed colour, and fayd,
" My poor little ones ! muft I leave them fo
foon ? "   She covered her eyes with her hands
for a minute, and I faw her lips moving.
Then fhe went to their little Bed where
they lay warmly afleep, lockt in each other's
arms, like the Princes in the Tower, and
kiffed 'em both.   The biggeft fleepily fayd,
" Good night."   She fayth, " Good night.
God blefs my children."

Lettice had made up her little Fardel, and
gave it her weeping.   She took the good
Girl about the Neck and kiffed her, faying,
" Be a Mother to my Children."   " O Madam.,
you will come back," fayd I.   " That is as may
be," quod fhe.   " We have not the ordering
of it."   We went forthe into the Dark, fhe
carrying her Bible : and took fhort cuts acrofs
fields and over ftiles we had learnt to know
by daylight, till we came to a lone Cottage.
Direftly we tapped, the door was opened, and
by no other than Sir Francis.   She fayd, " O
my Brother ! " and fell into his arms.

He kiffed her once or twice, and fayd
with emotion, " 'Tis well you are in fafety,
Nan ; you know not what I have fuffered.
Ye are emperilling me as well as yourfelf.

Now, keep quite cloſe in this place, till I bid you."

She ſayd, " I will."

" And you, Nicholas, return whence ye came." I heſitated.

She ſayd, " O yes, go back, Nicholas, and watch over the Children. Let me think they are cared for."

I ſighed and ſayd, " I obey."

" And now, fare thee well, Nan," ſayd Sir Francis. " Maybe ye are in leſs danger than I, when all's ſayd. I would that Woemen took more heed of conſequences."

" In which world ? " quod ſhe.

" Tut, tut," ſayd he, impatiently ; " there is a way that ſeems good unto a woman, but the end thereof is death."

She looked earneſtlie at him, and ſayd—

" Rather Death, than falſe of Faith."

He haſted forth, and preſentlie we heard a horſe galloping away. Then after a tender parting, I quitted her, ſhe begging me to let her know in a week, or ten days at moſt, how the Children were, and how things went. So I left her in that ſequeſtered place.

'Twas none too ſoon, for next morn I

was fitting indoors, with my Eyes but not my Mind on a Book, when two ftrange Men, marvelloufly fufpicious in appearance, came to the Door, and afked for Miftrefs Anne. The children by good hap were abroad with Lettice.

I pretended not to know who they meant ; and fayd, "There is no Miftrefs Anne here. Walk in and fee." For we had hidden away all her things. They fayd, "Who lodges here, then ?"

I fayd, "I do, with my Niece and two Children. I am a poor Scholar, revifing a Book. Perhaps you will like to buy it ?"

"What is it touching ? The Bible ?"

"No : the Adornment of Gardens."

They fcoffed ; and looked about the place a little, but found nothing. I watched them depart and took heart.

I waited the given time, and then went to fee her. To my confternation fhe was gone ! I afked the Purblind old Woeman whither fhe had fled. She fayd, to the Houfe in the Chalk-pit. How had fhe gone ? On a Pillion behind a Man.

I was troubled and difmayed, and afkt the diftance. Five mile, or maybe fomething better. How long had ſhe been gone? Two days.

I ſtarted off at once, and reached the Houſe in the Chalk-pit footſore and wearie. It was ſhut up and ſparred within : I knocked : a fierce Maſtiff raged inſide, but ſeemed the only living Creature. In vain I cried and ſhouted. I gat no anſwer.

Turning aſide in ſorrow of heart, I ſaw a little boy peering at me through a Hedge. I ſayd, "My pretty Boy, haſt thou ſeen a Lady about here?" He ſayth, "Aye." "Where is ſhe gone?" "With ſome Men." "Where have they ta'en her?" "To the Houſe i' th' Wood." "How were the Men apparelled?" "In blue coats and badges." "What was on the Badges?" "An aſs." Then I was comforted, for 'twas the Aſkew cognizance. I ſayd, "Canſt take me to the Houſe i' th' Wood?" He heſitated, till l promiſed him a guerdon. Then he ſet off running before me on his bare feet, till I could hardlie follow. Howſoe'er, I managed to keep him in ſight.

At length, he was ſpent, and cried, "See ye that foot-track thro' the brake! Follow it : I cannot go farther." I urged him, but he was

9*

footſore and breathleſs, ſo I gave him the
Penny and followed the Path.   It proved
much longer and more devious than he had
told me, and I oft had to fight my way through
briars, and ſometimes I feared I had been ſent
aſtray by a villanous Child.

At length I came out on a little Glade, and
on the farther ſide of it, ſure enow, was the
Houſe i' th' Wood.   A Hunting-lodge, ſeem-
inglie, fallen into decay ; ſome of the ſhutters
hanging by one hinge ; but a thin wreath of
ſmoke curling from a chimney betokened occupation.   There was a little Brook between me
and it ; and the banks being rather ſteep, I
could not eaſily croſs.   While walking along
its Margent, looking for a ford, I heard the
ſtealthy footfall of Horſes, and peeping
through the buſhes, watched to ſee who ſhould
come.

Acroſs the Glade, beyond the Houſe, was a
narrow road conſiſting of little but two ruts
o'ergrown with graſs.   From the covert of
Wood over this road iſſued forthe a little knot
of horſemen : one of the foremoſt being Sir
Francis.   He was wrapped in a black cloak ;
his uſually fair and florid face was ſickly pale,
his air creſtfallen.   They halted and looked to

him for direction: he ſeemed irreſolute a
moment—then, waving his daſtard arm toward
the Houſe, wheeled his horſe about and
galloped out of ſight. The Craven!—the fell
Traytour!

In deſperation, I leaped the Brook; fell,—
ſprained myſelf,—yet ran limping to the back
premiſes and battered at the Door, crying,
"Alarm! alarm!" None heard me. There
was a confuſed ſound of voices in front; I ran
round, and ſaw them lifting Miſtreſs Anne on
to a horſe.

I know not what I cried, but ſhe looked
about; and without bewraying me for her follower, cried out, "Farewell, all who love me!
I go to ſhort pain and long joy."

I ruſhed at them, and cried, "Take me too
—I'm the ſame as ſhe! If ſhe's guilty, I'm
guilty."

But they only laughed.

"Give the good Man a lift thro' the Wood,"
ſayd ſhe, calmly. "He hath been a faithful
ſervitor."

"Clamber up behind me, then," ſayd one of
the horſemen to me, not unkindlie. With
thankfulneſs I obeyed.

Soon we were threading the wood in ſingle

file, but when we got out on a wider road, I
prayed my companion to let me ride alongside
Miſtreſs Anne, which, however, he would
not.

And ſo we rode on Londonward, I wot not
how long, being ſicke with griefe, till we came
to a branch road, when my companion ſayd,
" Alight now.   In faith, thou haſt had a pretty
good lift."

And Miſtreſs Anne, looking round, cried,
" Farewell ! farewell !"

O how beautiful ſhe looked, and how ſweet
and thrilling was her voice !   I ſtrained mine
eyes after her as long as ſhe was in ſight, and
then went on my way weeping.

That craven Brother !   How I hated him
in my heart !   He had indeed, as I learnt
afterwards, been aſſayled with threats that
might intimidate a Cowardly nature, which
his was now proven to be ; but that excuſed
him not from leading the Myrmidons of
injuſtice himſelf to the Retreat he only knew
of and had placed her in, with the promiſe
of Safety.   Oh, 'twas villanous !   No Plume
wore he in his ſlouched hat that day,
but he ſhowed moſt compleatly the white
Feather.

But mark the reſult to himſelf. Men may diſplay their natural badneſs an' they will, being led captive by the Deſtroyer, but Juſtice ſets her mark on them ſometimes, in a manner that ſhows beyond miſtake the Divine diſpleaſure. From the hour he pointed out her Aſylum and then fled like a timid Hare, he ſaw ever before him, e'en to the Day of her Death, an inſufferable bright Light, which he ſpoke of as like that of a great and horrible Fire reflected in a glaſs Window. This curſe he took about him, wherever he went, do what he would, and ſometimes it drew from him Groans and Tears of torment.

When I got back to the Cottage, I found Lettice and the Infants gone! I ſhould now have been bewildered outright, but for a billet left for me by my Niece, bidding me not to be alarmed, for that the Babes had been ſent for by Miſtreſs Diſney, who would ſuccour them till rejoined by their Mother.

The Neſt being thus reft of its Fledglings, I turned my back on the Cottage next morning (for my fatigue and grief inſiſted on a few hours' reſt), and took my way back to

Temple Bar, where I craved ſhelter from
Miſtreſs Berry. The good ſoul readilie
took me in, bidding me lodge and table
with her, free of charge, as long I behoved,
and ſhed ſad tears on hearing of this new
Trouble.

Then I went to Maſter Britain, and he
told me Miſtreſs Anne was in ward; but
that Kyme was going to appear before her
firſt, and charge her with forſaking him.
Sure, this was the Wolf charging the Lamb
with muddying the Stream; for had he not
turned her out of Doors?

Maſter Britain's Clerk, i' the outer Chamber, whom I knew pretty well by this
time, ſayd as I came out, "Pauſe awhile,
I have ſomething to give you,"—and went
away.

Almoſt the next moment, Sir Francis
paſſed through, and went ſtraight in to
Maſter Britain. I ſhrank back with inward
loathing, but he noticed me not. His face
looked wan and ſhrunk, his eyes continuallie
blinked as though he could not controule the
vibration of his eyelids. I heard him, in
moſt piteous and lamentable guiſe, pray
Maſter Britain to get his Siſter off, even

at the price of half his Fortune. Maſter
Britain ſayd he ſhould do his beſt at any
rate, but theſe were matters not to be reached
by Guerdon. He ſeemed to wonder at
Kyme's thinking of turning the tables on
her; but Sir Francis' thoughts were all
of the Eccleſiaſtical Court. My blood boiled
when I heard the craven Knight avow
ſuch concern for her, and never let fell that
'twas he led the Myrmidons to her Retreat.
"Waking or ſleeping," ſayth he, "I get no
Reſt."

Involuntarilie the words eſcaped me, as
though forcing 'emſelves from my heart—

"Rather Death than falſe of Faith."

He inſtantly gave a kind of Sob, and I
heard a heavy Fall. Maſter Britain called,
"Help! help!" I ran in, and ſaw Sir
Francis on the floor.

"Run, run for a Doctor!" cried Maſter
Britain. I did ſo, and in the doorway nearly
ran againſt the Clerk, carrying a big Book he
thought I ſhould find good reading. He told
me where to find ye neareſt Leech, with
whom I returned; and finding Sir Francis
was alreadie recovering from his Swoon, I
paſſed out, not wiſhing to ſee or hear more of

him. I was difmayed at the effect of my fo hafty Ejaculation, which prickt too fore a Confcience. He took the echo of his Sifter's words for fupernatural. Mafter Britain, not knowing 'em to be hers, nor coupling them with the Trance, nor even catching their fub-ftance, did only think of Sir Francis' o'er-wrought condition, and attribute it to fheer Affection and Attendriffement.

Now we were all at Paufe till Mafter Kyme fhould arrive in London. When he did fo, fhe was brought before the Privy Council without further delay, and accufed of refufing, without juft caufe, to live with her husband. When plied with Queftions, fhe refufed to anfwer them, faying the Lord Chancellor alreadie knew all about it : and when he told her it was the Royal pleafure fhe fhould plead, fhe defired to do fo before the King in per-fon.

"It is not reafon," he reply'd, "that the King fhould be troubled on your account."

"And yet," quod fhe, "the wifeft King that ever lived refufed not to hearken unto two poor women that came to him for juftice."

In fine, they could make nothing of it,

Kyme's cafting her forthe being a fact that could not be denyed ; and neither of 'em being minded to rehearfe the previous words that had paffed between them.

So Mafter Kyme returned unto his own Place ; and then the more dangerous charge of Herefy was brought againft her. Firft, Wriothefley afked her of her opynyon of the Sacrament ; to whom fhe gave no direct anfwer ; and when Gardiner did charge her to fpeak out, fhe fayd—

"I will not fing a new fong unto the Lord in a ftrange land."

Then enfewed a fharp argument betwixt them, he accufing her of fpeaking in parables. Then fhe : " It is beft I fhould ; for if I fpeak the bare Truth, you will not receive it."

" You are a Parrot !" quod he ; which was a fingular contradiction to Bonner's complaynt of her that fhe was a woman of few words. To this check, fhe only made anfwer : " My Lord, I am willing to receive all things at your hands, whether Rebukes or what not."

One fhould think this might have foftened him ; but one after another of the Council did affayl and browbeat her ; prolonging the fitting to about five hours. Miftrefs Anne was then conveyed, much wearied, by the Clerk of the Council to my Lady Garnifh.

What paffed next day, when fhe was agayn brought before the Privy Council, I can but adduce, as above, from her own words. My Lord Chancellor agayn queftioned her as touching the Sacrament. She alleged fhe could onlie fay what fhe had alreadie fayd. After manie words, they bade her ftep afide. Lord Lifle, Lord Effex, and the Bifhop of Winchefter then fued her earneftly to profefs the bread and wine to be verily and indeed bone, flefh, and blood.

" It is a great fhame of you," fayd fhe, " to counfel contrary to your knowledge."

The Bifhop wifhed to fpeak with her in private ; but fhe refufed ; faying, " In the mouth of two or three witneffes, everything fhall be eftablifhed."

Then fayd the Lord Chancellor, " I muft have another word on the Elements." Quod fhe, " How long will you halt, my Lord, on both ? "

" Where found you that ? " fayd he. She anfwered, " In the Scripture."

" You will be burnt," quod the Bifhop. Well, well," fayd fhe, " I have fearched all the Scriptures, yet never could find that either Chriſt or His Apoſtles ever put anie creature to death."

They would have obtayned her ſignature to a paper, but this ſhe refuſed.

SECTION XIV.

Delivered to ye Tormentors.

ITHERTO Miſtreſs Anne's Courage had never quelled, nor her
Faith waxed weak. But it pleaſes
God to teſt and prove r .is ſervants,
that they may know all theire ſtrength to be
from Him, and that without Him they are
nothing.

When I returned to Miſtreſs Berry's, after
picking up what I coulde of the Examination
at Greenwich, who ſhould I find there but my
Niece, Lettice! She, ſeeing my ſurpriſe,
ſayd, "Maſter Kyme hath diſcharged me,
refuſing anie payment of Wages ſince the
Night I left his Houſe and followed Miſtreſs
Anne."

"Nay," ſayd I, "that was to be expected."

"And ſince," purſued Lettice, "Miſtreſs
Diſney hath undertaken the Children, and
declines my being about them, I came
hither to ſee if perchance I might be permitted to wait on my deare Lady."

At this moment, there came in Lady
Denny's man Chriſtopher, who had often
attended Miſtreſs Anne from Court, and
brought Letters and Meſſages ; and meſeemed he looked kindlie on my Niece.
This impreſſion was not weakened by the
Start I ſaw him give, when he entered and
found her with me.

"You here, Miſtreſs Lettice ? " quod he.
"How I wiſh you could be placed about
your miſfortunate Lady."

"That is the ſame thing which I covet,"
ſayd Lettice. "Do ye think, Sir, it can be
brought about ? "

"Nay, I know not," returned he ; "but
this I know, that it would give entire pleaſure
to my Lady ; and with your approval I will
name it to her and aſk whether it may be
done."

"Do ſo, by all means," ſayd Lettice ; and

then, after detailing each to each all we knew
and had ſeen of this ſad Buſineſſe, he made as
though to leave, but yet ſtepped back from
the Door to notice ſome pretty Flower in
the little Court behind, and drew Lettice
out to tell him its name ; and there I thought
they had a little Lover's Talk, ſuch as the
ſtaid think fooliſh, but which I diſapproved
not for either, they being ſo diſcreete and
good.

At length it grew dark, and I thought
the talk laſted too long ; and when I looked
forthe I ſaw them ſtill in the Doorway, their
heads cloſe together, and I cryed, " 'Tis nigh
the time when ſober Folk ſhut up."

" I come, Uncle," returned Lettice ſomewhat pettiſhly.

. " I go, Sir," ſayd Chriſtopher, yet went
not.

Then I misjudged 'em both as elder folk
ſometimes do misjudge the young (not but
what Chriſtopher was turned of thirty) and
held the chamber door in my hand, half
minded to ſpeak agayn ; and ſoe heard,
ſoftly ſpoken, ſuch words as, " Well then,
good night . . . you promiſe . . . " " Yes, I
promiſe . . . " " You fully underſtand . . . "

" I fully underſtand . . . " " I may tell my
Lady ? " " You may." " Be ſecret." " As
the Grave." " Forget not the Signal." " As
ſoon forget my Prayers."

I e'en fancied a kiſs exchanged ; and
therein may have misjudged 'em too. Howbeit, when Lettice came in, and ſtruck a
light, I obſerved a bright hue on her cheek
and ſparkle in her eyes, which yet bore
traces of tears. I ſayd,—

" Ye are young, my Laſs ; and I ſtand to
thee in place of Father and Mother. Beware
of men . . . ſubtle poiſon is under their
tongues."

" Not ſuch tongues as yours, Uncle, nor
yet as Chriſtopher's," ſayth ſhe quickly.
" What think ye we were talking of ? Plans
of communication, in caſe I ſhould be ſhut
up with my Lady, and which e'en may lead
to her releaſe."

The good Creatures ! How badly I had
misjudged 'em !

Now, at this very time, as we afterwards
learnt, Miſtreſs Anne lay in Ward at Greenwich, ſorrowful unto Death . . . all her
Courage gone, her Faith quenched, her
Heart diſmayed, her Fears raging, her Sins

brought back upon her, like a burthen too
heavy to bear ; a dark Cloud interpofed between her and her Saviour, and a great fear
of death taking hold of her.   That was the
dread hour of the Powers of Darkneffe : her
foul refufed comfort, fhe watered her couch
with tears, and befought piteoufly fhe might
fee Mafter Latimer.   Infteade of which were
onlie Adverfaries and bufy Mockers.

Chriftopher came next day in great difmay
to tell us this ; and he fayd intereft was being made by fecret friends to get Lettice
admitted to her.

This was on a Sunday ; and we wreftled
in Prayer for her almoft all the Day, fince
fhe was brought too low to be able to pray
for herfelf.   Mark the anfwer.

In the height of her illnefs, when fhe
thought fhe fhould die, fhe was removed to
Newgate.   There, her ftrength was renewed
from above, never more to give way.   Her
enemies fearing fhe fhould 'fcape them by
too eafy an end, fo far relaxed as to let her
Maid vifit her from time to time.   When
fhe faw Lettice firft come in, fhe flung her
arms about her, and refted her head on her
neck.

" Oh," fayth fhe, " I have had a bitter fea-
fon of defolation, but it is clean overpaft.
My Lord fmiles upon me : He will not hide
His face agayn."

She now wrote to her friends, begging
them to pray for her. And fhe wrote to
the King, meekly fetting forth the articles
of her Faith, and affirming that, though by
nature finfull, yet fhe could take Heaven to
record fhe was innocent of all Herefy.

Next day, they brought her for examination to the Crown Inn, where Rich and
Bonner with all their power and fpecioufe
words went about to perfuade her to unfay
herfelf, but in vayn. After them, Dr.
Nicholas Shaxton counfelled her to recant
as he had done ; but fhe told him, " It had
been better for you, had ye ne'er been born."
Thereafter fhe was fent to the Tower.

At three o' the clock that fame Afternoon,
came to her Wriothefley and Rich, and it is
not to be doubted, at the immediate inftance
of the King, whofe jealoufie of his good
Queen's orthodoxie had now been artfullie
awakened by her Enemies, who defired to
bring her and fundrie of her Ladies to the
Block.

To this end the Lord Chancellor and Mr. Solicitor Generall now came, refolving by all Means, faire or foul, to get Miftrefs Anne to criminate them. They plied her with queftions as touching the Duchefs of Suffolk, Lady Suffex, Lady Hertford, Lady Denny, and Lady Fitzwilliam, but fhe fayd fhe had nothing to allege againft anie of them.

" Nay but," quod they, " the King hath been informed that ye can, an' if ye will, name a large number of perfons of the fame way of thinking as yourfelf."

" The King," fhe replyed, " hath beene mifinformed on that point, as on others, by thofe about him."

" Who affifted you in prifon ? "

" My maid, Sirs, went out and begged of the City Prentices, who gave her of their charitie, but who the good lads were I know not."

" Nay, but we know ye had money of certayn Ladies, whofe names ye can tell if ye will."

" Indeed, a man in a blue coat did once bring me ten fhillings, as he fayd, from Lady Hertford ; and another in a violet coat gave me eight fhillings, he fayd, from Lady

Denny. But in faith, Sirs, 'tis like the good man gave it me of his own good will."

"What members of the Privy Council contributed to your needs in Priſon?"

"Not one."

"'Tis falſe!" burſt forthe the Chancellor; "and unlefs ye give up their names ye ſhall be racked."

"I have no names to give up."

Then they ſummoned Sir Thomas Knyvet, Lieutenant of the Tower, to ſubject her tender body to that villanous Torture. . . . Oh! what ſayth Scripture? "I ſay unto you, my friends, Fear not them which can deſtroy the Body, but afterwards have no more that they can do."

She did not fear! ſhe, ſo lately overwhelmed with Tears and Terrors, now meekly ſubmitted herſelf to the Tormentors, and uttered no Moan. Sir, in their deviliſh ſpight, they had doubtlefs thought to delight their ears with her weeping Lamentaçions; and becauſe ſhe now fuſtayned that horrid ſtretching with intrepid conſtancy, and ſtill gave up no names, thofe Beaſts rather than Men flung off their Gowns and racked her with their owne hands, till ſhe was well-nigh dead, yet after recover-

ing a little fhe reafoned with Wriothefiey on
the Sacrament, two hours off and on, and
yielded not one jot of the truth as fhe held it.

Now thefe things could not be done in a
corner, for fervants fpy out all theire Mafters'
ways ; and Chriftopher being in communication with Rich's fervant, had time to bring us
word of this long ordeal, and carry Lettice and
me down to the Tower, to fee what might hap.

Miftrefs Anne was then being carryed into
a private Houfe to be recovered, thofe Savages
being fomewhat fhamed at having fo mangled
her as nearly to be her Death ; and Chriftopher, knowing one of the Servants, did
fmuggle us in to minifter to her.

As I bent over her white, cold face, fhe
whifpered, " Sure, dear Friend, I have as
wearie and painful limbes as ever had patient
Job." I fayd, "O, dear Ladye, ye have fhown
Job's patience, and ye have Job's God to be
your Strength." "Aye, and He doth ftrength-
en me," whifpered fhe.

Some one of the houfe here brought in
word from the Chancellor, that if fhe would
recant, fhe fhoulde be mercifullie dealt with ;
but if fhe did refufe, fhe fhould be fent back
to Newgate and burnt.

She made anſwer, "Rather Death than falſe of Fayth."

To Newgate, therefore, ſhe was agayn committed, ſo ſoone as ſhe could be moved.

Meanwhile Sir Thomas Knyvet, in the greateſt trouble of mind, ſought the King's preſence, and humblie beſought his forgiveneſs for not having racked Miſtreſs Anne as extremely as the Chancellor and Mr. Secretary would have had him do.

The King, aſhamed of what had been done, forgave him, and bade him return to his charge ; and afterwards upbraided Wriothefley and Rich for their "extreme handling of the woman." And yet it was ſhrewdly ſuſpected he had authorized it himſelf! *Put not your faith in Princes.*

Now in Newgate at this time there was a little army of Martyrs in the ſame condemnation with Miſtreſs Anne, and deſtined for the ſame diſmal fate ; albeit one of them, George Blaage, being the King's ſervant, was let off. To Laſcelles, one of theſe priſoners, whom Miſtreſs Anne held in much eſteem, ſhe, as ſoon as able to uſe a pen, did indite the Letter here following :—

"O Friend moſt dearlie beloved in God!

"I marvel not a little what ſhould move you to judge me in ſo ſlender a Faith as to fear Death, which is the end of all Miſery. In the Lord, I deſire you not to believe of me ſuch Weakneſs; for I doubt not God will perform His work in me, like as He hath begun.

"I underſtand the Council is not a little diſpleaſed, that it is reported abroad that I was racked in the Tower. They ſay now, that what they did there was but to fear me; whereby I perceive they are aſhamed of their uncomely Doings, and fear much leſt the King's Majeſty ſhould have information thereof; wherefore they would that no Man ſhould noiſe it. Well, theire crueltie God forgive them!"

Indeed ſhe wrote manie godlie letters during her few remayning days, to ſtrengthen and refreſh our Souls with that Comfort wherewith ſhe was comforted. As alſo, a full declaration of her faith, which if Time and occaſion ſerve, I will put in an Appendix.

But now the doom went forth that die

fhe fhould; and by that moft horrid Payn of Burning. Along with her were to fuffer, firfte, a Shropfhire Prieft, called Nicholas Belenian; next, Mafter John Lafcelles, Gentleman of the Houfehold to the King's Majefty; third, John Adams, a fimple Tailor: widely differing from one another in all Outward Circumftances; all alike in the Communion of Faith.

Within her iron Cage, ye might then have heard our fweet Bird finging a hymn of her own compofure, ending with—

Yet, Lord, I Thee defire:
For that they do to me,
Let them not tafte the hire
Of their Iniquitie.

SECTION XV.

Adjutor in Tribulationibus.

IT would be impoffible to defcribe the awful Rumour through London ftretes, the Night afore the Martyrdom. It was fixed for the third Day after the laft Examination. Miftrefs Berry, all bewept, would faine have me take her beforehand to Smithfield, where the dreadful Tragedy was to be brought to its Clofe; and many Citizens and their Wives, unable to bear the dread Spectacle itfelf, were minded to fee the Spot, as well as a multitude of the bafer fort, who love to be ftimulated with whatever is horrible.

Thus, as we approached the place, we found it almoſt impaſſable; but yet were let through when 'twas under-ſtood we had perſonal concern in one of the Martyrs; and pitying looks were given us, with murmurs of "Poor ſoules."

We coulde hear the hollow Reverbe-ration of many Hammers uſed by the Carpenters who were buſilie ſetting up a raiſed and covered Stage in front of St. Bartholomew's Hoſpital, whereon the Lord Chancellor and his Com-peers were to ſit; alſo a temporary Pulpit for the Sermon to the con-demned; and round all, a ſtrong, circu-lar Fence, incloſing a good area. Right in the centre, before the Stage and no great ſpace from the Pulpit, were alreadie to be ſeen three ſtrong Oaken Stakes, with a Pile of Fagots beſide them; at the mere ſight of which, many women wept, turned ſick, and were readie to faint. We met manie puſhing away from it, whoſe places were eagerly filled by new Comers.

Having rent our hearts by this ſad ſcene, I took Miſtreſs Berry out of the crowd, and went ſtraight to Newgate, having gotten a Paſs.

I found Miſtreſs Anne ſewing a button to the collar of the long white garment ſhe was to wear on the morrow, and biting off the Thread as I had oft ſeene her do in happier hours. She raiſed her Angel Face, which was as calm as if ſhe were preparing for ſome Chriſtian feſtival, and holding out her hand, ſayd,—

"O, dear Friend, how it joys me to ſee you! Do not go to Smithfield to-morrow—it will tax you too ſorelie. My light Affliction, which will be but for a Moment, will. lead to a far more exceeding and Eternal Weight of Glory."

I ſayd, " How *can* you call it light ? "

" Becauſe the Lord makes it ſo," ſhe replyed. " He ſank beneath His own Croſs : but He takes up the heavie End of mine. And thus, my Burthen is light."

Seeing I could not anſwer her for Tears, ſhe ſayd, "Come, I will ſing to you . . ."

" Oh, do not—do not ! . . ."

"Yes, let me, for the laſt time, Nicholas! —till I ſing the Lord a new Song in his bleſſed Kingdom. I made words and tune myſelf, as I ſewed at my Shroud ; now hear how goodly it is."

And herewith ſhe took one of my hands in both her own, and though ſo wrenched by that vile Rack that ſhe could not ſet foot on the Ground, ſhe looked in my face, and ſmiled and ſang till I almoſt wiſhed to die hearing her ſo ſing. Then ſhe ſayd, "Let us pray." And prayed for us all, and for her Ene-myes, and laſt for herſelf. "Now, you pray," quod ſhe ; and ſo I did. I wot not how long we ſhould have gone on this way, but that Archdeacon Louth came to viſit her ; ſo I had to take leave of her, he over-looking us, and could not, for Manhood and Chriſtianitie, ſhow leſs fortitude than ſhe, who had ſuch need to retayn her ſelf com-mand. She kiſſed me, once and agayn, calling me her father, bade me give her love to Lettice, and Miſtreſs Berry, and all in-quiring friends ; then waved me off, ſtill ſmiling, with—

"Now go : I have another to ſee : good

bye ! good bye !—Have a care of your
health, Nicholas !   We fhall meet agayn !" ...
The Archdeacon looked on, aftonied.

SECTION XVI.

Freed at Laſt.

FTER her bidding me ſpare myſelf, and not go, ye may wonder that I went—— Sir ! I coulde not refrayn. I muſt needs catch the laſt ſight of her. But what ! Could I not bear to ſee, what ſhe could bear to ſuffer ?

I hired a window in a mean Houſe o'er-looking Smithfield Market, the owner being a ſecret Friend of Miſtreſs Anne's, or, at any rate, of ſome of her fellow-ſufferers To this place I repaired overnight, which they told me would be neceſſarie, becauſe of the preſs. And they offered me Supper and Bed ; but I would not ſuffer mine eye-lids to take reſt, nor partake aught ſave the bread of affliction and the water of affliction.

If her Friends could not wreftle for her in Prayer, that night, and all night long, what manner of Friends muft they be? Had I e'en been minded to fleep, the lugubrious noifes outfide, and *fufurra* of the mixed Multitude, muft have prevented it. Early in the morning, the church Bell began to toll with a heavie, difmal found. A body of Halbardiers came and encircled ye fence. Before it well got light, I faw men bufie piling the Fagots about the Stakes, and carefully inferting fomewhat among them. I afked the Owner of the Houfe what they were about. He fayd, putting refinous matters, and, maybe, gunpowder, to fhorten the Martyrs' fuffering. Therein I took fome comfort.

At length, after much fufpenfe, a general movement and fuppreffed hum told that the prifoners were approaching. The Lord Chancellor, old Duke of Norfolk, Earl of Bedford, and Lord Mayor, arrived with much Pomp, and took their feats, which had now a red awning. A ftrange, confufed moan or groan from many voices, arofe as the Martyrs came in, with bare heads and feet, and in long white Garments. Inaſmuch as, by reaſon of her previous racking, Miſtreſs Anne could not ſtand, ſhe was brough in a Cart, containing a Chair, in which ſhe was ſupported by two Sergeants at Arms. My eyes grew miſty as they lifted her out, and when I could look at her agayn, ſhe was bound with a chain to the ſame ſtake with another of the four Martyrs; and Fagots were being heaped about them. Then there was a Pauſe.

And now the weak-hearted Shaxton mounted the Pulpit, and began to inveigh againſt the pure doctrine which, not long agone, he himſelf had upheld. I doubt if a ſingle ſoul attended to his Sermon, ſave Miſtreſs Anne, who, when he grievouſly miſ-quoted Scripture, ſayd, in her clear, ſilver voice, "He ſpeaketh without the Book." I ſaw the Chancellor gnaw his nails at this.

And next the tempting offer of the King's written pardon, as unfolded and diſplayed by the Chancellor, was made to each Martyr in turn. Miſtreſs Anne refuſed even to look at it, ſaying, "I am not come here to deny my

Lord and Mafter." The others refufed in
turn. Whereon my Lord Mayor rofe in his
place, and in a loud, deep voyce, cried,

"*Fiat Juftitia,*"

and immediately the fagots began to
crackle.

Now there was a great fwaying to and fro
of the crowd, as of a mighty Wave of the
Sea, and I believe there were cryings and
moanings, and favage ftrugglings for places.
Amidft it all, my Lord Chancellor rofe up
in great hafte, along with all his Compeers,
and with moft ungraceful Diforder would
have quitted the Stage ; having heard there
was Gunpowder amongft the Stakes, and
fearing the Explofion might reach 'em.
Some time elapfed, ere they were fatiffyed
on this point and refumed their Places.

Clouds of white, eddying Smoke, and
darting forks of Flame, now concealed the
Martyrs from our eyes ; but thofe neareft to
them heard them utter pious Ejaculations.
The Smoke parting a little, I faw deare
Miftrefs Anne's head fallen on her cheft,
and felt affured fhe was fmothered. The

next inſtant, a loud Report cauſed a general
outcry : the powder had exploded. Their
light Affliction, which was but for a Moment,
had been exchanged for a far more exceeding
and eternal Weight of Glory.

Sir, they ſay there was a Thunder-ſtorm
burſt over us at the time, but I was too
abſorbed to note it. To me, the whole
world had, for the nonce, become a blank.
That night, ſtrange to ſay, I ſlept heavilie.
During the evening, I and Lettice, and
Miſtreſs Berry and Chriſtopher, had gathered
together and communed on all that lay in
our Hearts. We were ſenſible of an inex-
preſſible Load taken off us ; the worſt had
been done. It could never be done agayn :
ſhe was beyond and above their reach now.
We wept, and talked of her pretty ways, and
how we had feared once and agayn her
courage might fayl at the End. But it never
did.

That night, I learned that Chriſtopher
had aſked Lettice to be his Wife. I ſayd,
" I can entruſt you with her ; I know her
happineſſe will be in ſafe keeping. But let
us not think of Wedding Bells along with
Martyr Fires."

To be brief: in due time they were marryed; they have been happy, and have reared up a numerous and virtuous progeny. I am always welcome at their Farm, and from time to time have ſtayed there; but I am now ſo well ſtricken in years,—though my Sight, Hearing, and Memory are unimpayred,—that I prefer hanging about the old Home of my Boyhood, where I hope, not longe hence, to die.

Sir, I have tried not to be garrulous; I have ſayd little or nothing of mine owne People—my good Father and Mother—their edifying Deaths, within a few Hours of one another—the death of Sir Maurice the Chaplain—my going up to Greenwich to preſent my Book to the King's Majeſty, &c.; and yet I fear I have mentioned myſelf nearlie as oft as Miſtreſs Anne.

This is a fault, and ſhould be correǒted. But I am too old for correǒtion now. It hath given me ſome pleaſure to jot down theſe fading Memoryes and read them afterwards to Jaſper . . . I have likewiſe journeyed to Chriſtopher's Farm, and read over the MS. to him and Lettice, now paſt their Meridian; it recalled ſome ſad yet ſweet recollections to them, in ſpecial including what firſt brought them together; viz., mutual concern for a moſt unfortunate Lady. And an eſteem baſed on ſuch a concern is very fit to be itſelf the baſe of a true and virtuous Love.

But what of Miſtrefs Anne's foes? They are all dead, and gone to their own place, wherever that may be. If there were anie thing to be alleged in their excuſe, I hope it will be alleged. God is not extreme to mark what is done amiſs, ſpecially from Ignorance. But there are ſome Sins that proceed from a worſe Root than that: from deſperate Hardneſs of Heart and Tyrannouſneſs. I believe there muſt be a condign Puniſhment for ſuch. I ſhould believe it, if 'twere not revealed; but it is. We are told of it by Him who was emphaticallie *The Truth*, and He was ſo ſorrie for what the unrepentant needs muſt come to, if they turned not, that He gave His own life for them, to the end that all who believe in Him ſhould not periſh, but have everlaſting Life.

In Stallingboro' Church, ye may ſee the fayre Tomb of marble, under which lie buried Sir William Aſkew and Dame

Margery, his fecond Wife. Upon the tomb is the portrayture of himfelfe, in compleat Armour ; upon his Surcoat his armes, Sa : a feffe d'or entre trois Affes paffants d'argent, maynes, tayles, and hoofs. . . . . There, alfo, ye may fee the tomb of Sir Francis, reprefented upon it by a recumbent half ftatue, his head forrowfullie reclining on his left hand. He died long ago, Sir, while I, his fenior, ftill live. His eldeft fon and heir, died before him.

I am not forrie to have been put upon making this brief abftrackt of a very forrowful Page of Family Hiftory, in fpecial at the requeft of a young Gentleman who may be advantaged by this Inftance of the Victory of the Soul over the Body ; as well as deterred from Pufillanimity by the fad falling off of the gallant and gracioufe Sir Francis.

But as to applying the fubftance of the Lincolnfhire Tragedy to the Stage . . albeit as full of dramatique Intereft as aught in Sophocles or Euripides, though the one wrote of Antigone and the other of Iphigenia . . . Sir, the fubject matter is too facred, and involves too frequent reference to Holy

names and ſymbols, that ſhould not be
brought on the Stage   A profane Hand
muſt not touch them

FINIS.